CONVENIENT MARRIAGE, SURPRISE TWINS

BY
AMY RUTTAN

First published in Great Britain 2017
By Mills & Boon, an imprint of Harper Collins*Publishers*
1 London Bridge Street, London, SE1 9GF

Large Print edition 2018

ISBN: 978-0-263-07248-8

MIX
Paper from
responsible sources
FSC® C007454

This book is produced from independently certified FSC™ paper to ensure responsible forest management. For more information visit www.harpercollins.co.uk/green.

Printed and bound in Great Britain
by CPI Group (UK) Ltd, Croydon, CR0 4YY

“This is for you.”

Lana took the box from him. “What is it?”

“Your engagement ring.”

She almost dropped the box. She set down her champagne flute and stared at the black velvet box. Something that was just fake was becoming too real right now.

As if sensing that she was nervous, Andrew took the box out of her hand, opened it and pulled out a beautiful square-cut diamond. He slipped it on her finger. His hands were so strong, while hers trembled.

“You’re shaking,” he said. He ran his thumb in a circle over her knuckles.

“I wasn’t expecting this.”

“Well, we *are* engaged. People expect to see a ring.”

“I suppose.” She glanced up at him and looked into his eyes. Those blue eyes that seemed to melt right into her very soul. His touch was nice. Just a simple touch made her feel alive.

“It’s a beautiful ring,” she whispered.

Andrew leaned over and spoke into her ear. “Not as beautiful as the hand it graces.”

She didn’t know what to say to that. No one had ever paid her a compliment like that before. It caught her off guard and she felt as if she was frozen to the spot. She was certainly frozen in the moment, her pulse racing, trembling and yearning for his touch.

Lana realized she was holding her breath, waiting for a kiss…

Dear Reader,

Thank you for picking up a copy of *Convenient Marriage, Surprise Twins*—my 15th Mills and Boon Medical Romance! I can't believe it's been fifteen books. It still feels as if I sold my first one yesterday.

This book was so much fun to write because of the characters—I have a soft spot for Canadian heroes—and because of the setting. I've never been to Hawaii, but it's on my bucket list. I had a lot of fun researching Oahu and Waikiki, as well as surfing.

Surfing is fascinating to me. I would never try it, because I'm not the most brilliant swimmer and I'm terrified of sharks, but it was enjoyable living vicariously through my characters.

Dr Lana Haole and I have a lot in common—except the surfing thing—but I share a lot of similarities with Dr Andrew Tremblay as well. These characters are meant for each other, but they're too stubborn to see it, and sometimes I can be too stubborn to see things too. Just ask my husband…or maybe not!

This book is also special because it was the last book I worked on with my former editor Laura, so it's a little bittersweet for me. She's been there for fourteen of my books and has made me a better writer in every way.

I hope you enjoy Lana and Andrew's story.

I love hearing from readers, so please drop by my website amyruttan.com or give me a shout on Twitter @ruttanamy.

With warmest wishes,

Amy Ruttan

Born and raised just outside Toronto, Ontario, **Amy Ruttan** fled the big city to settle down with the country boy of her dreams. After the birth of her second child Amy was lucky enough to realise her lifelong dream of becoming a romance author. When she's not furiously typing away at her computer she's mum to three wonderful children who use her as a personal taxi and chef.

Books by Amy Ruttan

Mills & Boon Medical Romance

Royal Spring Babies

His Pregnant Royal Bride

Hot Latin Docs

Alejandro's Sexy Secret

The Hollywood Hills Clinic

Perfect Rivals...

Sealed by a Valentine's Kiss

His Shock Valentine's Proposal
Craving Her Ex-Army Doc

Visit the Author Profile page
at millsandboon.co.uk for more titles.

This book is dedicated to all my readers.
Thank you for reading my books
and making 15 books possible.

And to Laura, for our last book together.
I'll miss you!

Praise for
Amy Ruttan

'I recommend *Perfect Rivals*... as a place to start for those who haven't thought of trying the Medical line before, because this will be an absolute treat. I give it five stars because of the characters, the plot, and the fact I couldn't put it down... Please read this book—*stat!*'

—*Goodreads*

CHAPTER ONE

"HE'S AN IDIOT. I dislike him. There's no way in heck I'm going to work with him, let alone marry him!"

What Iolana failed to say was, *Dr. Andrew Tremblay may be an ass, but he's sexy as hell and all I want to do is throw him down and either kiss him or strangle him repeatedly.*

Her little brother didn't need to know that part.

No one did.

Or she'd lose her reputation. The one that she'd painstakingly rebuilt since David had left her heart in tatters two years ago. She needed to keep that reputation intact. It was bad enough that she was the daughter of the Chief of Surgery.

Being the daughter of the Chief of Surgery meant that she had to work even harder to prove herself. That she didn't get handouts.

"Come on, Lana, he's the best trainer and sports medicine guy that knows about surfing.

He's going to get me into the championships in a couple of months. I need him."

"No way, Keaka. There is no way." Iolana smiled to herself, using her brother Jack's Hawaiian name, which drove him nuts. Even though he used it when he was surfing.

Jack frowned and crossed his arms as he glared at her.

"There is no point in giving me the death stare, Keaka. I invented that death stare." Iolana pushed past him. And she had taught him that death stare. She'd practically raised Jack after their mother left.

"Dad would've applied for his green card as his employer."

"No, Dad didn't want to do that. He sees it as favoritism." Jack rolled his eyes. Lana didn't find it hard to believe that her father hadn't applied for Dr. Tremblay's green card. That sounded like something her father would do.

Never take responsibility, unless it was his patient or his hospital. Which was why Jack was here, begging her to fix his problem. Like she'd done before. Many times. Lana shouldered a lot of responsibility for her little brother.

"Why didn't Andrew take care of it? He has time."

"He got busy. Now it's too late for him."

Lana rolled her eyes.

Not surprising.

The moment Andrew had walked through the doors of Kahu Kai Hospital he'd had entitled, irresponsible playboy written all over him. Not irresponsible with his patients, but with everything else in his life.

"Keaka, I love you but I don't think so."

"Come on, Lana," Jack begged. "Andrew Tremblay was the best surfer for years. He dominated the world championships. I need this favor from you."

Iolana snorted. "A Canadian who was a world champion surfer. Seems highly unlikely."

"Don't judge a book by its cover, Lana!" There was a glint in Jack's eye and Iolana couldn't help but smile, just a bit, as she sat down on the edge of her desk, crossing her arms the way her little brother had done to give *him* the death stare.

Jack was younger than her by ten years and he always got what he wanted, being the only son. Lana had shouldered a lot of responsibility since their mother left. Their father was a prominent surgeon in Oahu, claiming that he was a distant descendant from an ancient king who ruled Oahu and didn't have time to raise little kids. So Lana had raised Keaka "Jack" Jr.

Iolana knew their father, Dr. Keaka Haole Sr., wanted Jack to follow in his footsteps and be a surgeon. Except Jack didn't want any of that. He wanted to be a world champion surfer. That was Jack's passion, and it had been Iolana's too, but there'd been such a gulf between Jack and her father since their mother left that Iolana felt as if she had to constantly work to repair the rift between them.

Which was why she was an orthopedic surgeon at her father's hospital. Or surfing alongside her brother.

"Why should I marry him?"

"Because he's my friend, a lot of Hawaiian entrants are counting on him, I'm your brother and…" Jack rubbed the back of his neck. "He'll be kicked out, Lana. There is no surfing in Canada."

Iolana cocked an eyebrow. "I believe there is."

"It's not the same, which is why he came here and became a legend." Jack ran his hand through his hair. "Lana, athletes come from all over North

America to train with Dr. Andrew Tremblay, which is why Dad let him have hospital privileges here."

"Don't remind me," Iolana griped.

She was all too aware that Dr. Andrew Tremblay was given privileges at her hospital, in her department, no less. The way he strutted around the halls, when he was actually here, drove her bonkers.

So smug. So sure of himself.

She'd always thought Canadians were supposed to be nice.

Jack was right. Andrew brought in a lot of money to their hospital and it would make a significant dent in their hospital profits if he left. And Jack might lose his chance at becoming a champion surfer.

Her dreams had been crushed to keep the peace; she couldn't let that happen to Jack.

"I think this is fraud," she said. "I don't relish jail time."

"You've known Andrew for some time. I think we can pull it off. Besides, isn't Dad always on your case about settling down?"

Iolana frowned. She hated it when her brother was right and their father had been on at her lately about settling down. And her father respected Andrew and knew what he brought into their hospital.

Her father would approve of her choice.

Would he?

Her father had approved of David and look how that turned out. She'd become the laughingstock of the hospital, falling for a womanizer like David.

Her father had been disappointed instead of consoling when it had ended.

People pitied her.

Poor Dr. Lana Haole.

She hated the pity. Hated that her reputation had been destroyed.

It would just be for a year or two. It wouldn't be all that horrible to marry him for convenience sake.

Jack was grinning at her, probably because he knew that he was wearing her down and she was going to say yes.

"He has to ask me," Iolana said. "That's my condition. If he wants the world to believe that we're an item and that this marriage is legitimate to protect his keister, he's going to have to get on one knee with a ring and ask me."

Jack winced. “A ring?”

“A ring.” Iolana got up and walked to the door of her office, giving her little brother a subtle hint that she wanted him to leave. “And a nice, big, expensive…”

The words died in her throat when she saw that Andrew was on the other side of the door, a hand raised as if he was about to knock. He grinned in that boyish way that simultaneously made her melt and grated on her nerves. How many times had they butted heads on the ER floor? And he always ended arguments with that smile which infuriated her.

“I see Jack’s spoken to you.”

Iolana crossed her arms and glared at him. All he did was grin. “Dr. Tremblay,” she acknowledged.

He slipped his hands into the pockets of his white lab coat and grinned, leaning forward. “You know, if you glare at me like that no one is going to believe that we’re supposed to be getting married.”

Iolana growled as he moved past her and into her office. She shut the door and stood in front of it, glaring both at her brother and Andrew.

Andrew cocked his eyebrow. "You don't look too happy about this arrangement."

"And what about this arrangement should I be happy about?" she demanded.

"I get to stay here and work. I get to continue on your brother's training."

"And why should that make me happy?" she asked.

"Oh, come now, Dr. Haole. You treasure me and my experience."

"Well, I'll leave you two to figure out the details of this arrangement," Jack said nervously as he walked toward the door. Iolana fixed him with an icy glare as he moved past her and slipped out into the hallway.

"Hey, Keaka, not a word to Dad!" she called out after her brother, before slamming the door again and facing her intended.

"Keaka, eh? You must be ticked off at him." Andrew didn't look at her. Instead he wandered around, looking at everything but avoiding eye contact with her. Which was safer for him because she was sure her look would grill him on the spot.

"I'm not happy about this, Dr. Tremblay." She marched to her desk and took a seat in her chair.

She wanted to put something solid between the two of them. She folded her hands on her desk. "There are stipulations to this arrangement."

He cocked one of those blond eyebrows of his and adjusted his glasses. "Stipulations?"

"You want this to be believable, don't you? I mean, if Immigration were to find out, our careers and the reputation of this hospital would be at stake. Jail time as well. Besides, I'm not irresponsible. *I* would've dealt with this long ago, so as not to resort to this."

He nodded, but she could tell by the way his lips were firmly pressed together he didn't enjoy her lecture. He just tolerated it. "Fair enough. What did you have in mind, Dr. Haole?"

"I want a public proposal," she said. "And I want a ring."

"You want a ring?" he asked in disbelief that wiped the haughtiness off his face.

"We have to make this as real as possible." Iolana couldn't help but grin. "I'm risking a lot."

"Is that so?" He leaned over her desk, those blue eyes of his boring into her. "Any particular cut?"

She held out her hand, wiggling her fingers in front of him and grinning, knowing that she was bugging him immensely. "I'm partial to an emerald cut, but I'll leave that up to you. There has to be some romance in this arrangement."

Andrew made a face. "Is there anything else?"

"Well, we're going to have to suss out living arrangements, I suppose. I guess it would make the most sense if you move in with me, and we'll have to sign a prenuptial agreement."

"It's not a real marriage," he said and then looked highly insulted. "What's wrong with my place?"

"Don't you live in an apartment? I have a house. And it is a real marriage—we're really getting married. It's not a make-believe marriage. I have to protect my assets."

"Fine." He straightened and crossed his arms. "So when am I supposed to make this public announcement of our engagement?"

"I'm not sure. Perhaps at the fund-raiser at the end of the week? That would be a good place for you to get down on one knee and give me a ring."

"You have this all figured out, and so fast." Andrew grinned then. "You're secretly pleased by this, aren't you? I think there's more to you than meets the eye."

Heat bloomed in her cheeks. “I think fast on my feet. That’s all.”

“No, I think you secretly want this. You want me.”

She was seeing red. “I could turn you in.”

“You won’t, though.”

“Won’t I?”

“No, because you’re attracted to me. You just don’t want to admit it.”

She glared at him. “Now I remember why I didn’t want to do this. You’re an arrogant jerk.”

“So why are you doing this if you detest me so?”

“Business. You bring revenue into this hospital.”

“That I can’t deny.” He grinned. “Is that all?”

No.

He was her ticket to have people stop pitying her. Including David.

“I love my brother and he thinks you’ll bring him to the surfing championships.”

Andrew nodded. “Jack is talented and he will get to the finals. He will be a champion.”

Iolana smiled then. “That’s why I’m doing it. Nothing more.”

"It is a lot for you to take on. You must love your brother."

"I do."

"Well, I appreciate it." And she knew that he meant it; just the change in his attitude made her think that he was sincere.

"Are you actually thanking me, Dr. Tremblay? I'm shocked."

"Don't get too used to it, Dr. Haole. And I think, because we're supposed to be intimate, we can drop the formalities and use our first names. I mean, people won't believe that we're madly in love if we refer to each other as Dr. Tremblay and Dr. Haole."

"Fine," Iolana said. Though the thought of being intimate, of letting her guard down made her stomach twist. David had hurt her so badly that the thought of letting someone else in, no matter how lonely she was, was terrifying indeed. Even if it was fake. It was risky.

Andrew grinned again. That charming smile. "So Lana, would you like to accompany me to the staff meeting?"

"Of course… Andrew."

She'd forgotten about the staff meeting with her father. She was in charge of Ortho and sports medicine, but her father was in charge of all the surgeons at Kahu Kai Hospital in Honolulu. Which was why she couldn't let another scandal rock her. It was bad enough people thought she was where she was because of who her father was.

Her father would be pleased with her choice of fiancé, but she doubted very much he would be pleased with the fact that Keaka, Andrew and her were all pulling a fast one on him. They were doing something illegal to keep Andrew in the country.

And it made her nervous to know that she'd be lying to her father.

That her father had a hold on her.

All because she wanted to keep the peace between him and Keaka.

They were late to the staff meeting. The other surgeons were waiting for them. She could feel her father's icy-cold stare boring into her as they stumbled in.

"Ah, Iolana and Andrew, thank you for joining us. You're fifteen minutes late," her father said, tapping his watch. "We all have schedules to keep."

Iolana opened her mouth to say something, but

Andrew stepped in front of her, taking her hand in his.

"I'm sorry, Dr. Haole, you can lay the blame solely on me." Then he grinned at her and she had a sinking feeling about what he was going to say next.

No. Don't you dare.

Only he didn't seem to get her telepathic message.

"You see, Dr. Haole, I've been dating your daughter for some time and we were delayed because I just got down on one knee and asked her to marry me."

Iolana plastered a fake smile on her face as the rest of the surgeons in the room, including her father, stared at them with their mouths hanging open. Even David was surprised, but then he smirked in disbelief. Which infuriated her.

"Iolana, is this true?" her father asked skeptically. And she knew he was thinking about David as well.

"Yes," she managed to say without breaking her very wide smile. "Yes. It is. I'm in love with Andrew, but we've kept our relationship a secret because of past experiences." She glared at

David, making him uncomfortable because he pulled at his collar.

Good.

Andrew slipped his arm around her and pulled her close. "I don't have to tell you what her answer is. It's obvious she said yes, and I know there's no ring yet, Dr. Haole, but there is one coming. I wanted to ask her to marry me at the fund-raising gala at the end of the week, but I just couldn't wait. I love your daughter so much."

"Yes," Iolana said. "Yes. We're so in love."

"You sound like a robot," Andrew whispered in her ear, but she ignored him.

"Well, let me be the first to congratulate you both," her father said and Iolana watched him cross the room to shake Andrew's hand, slapping him on the back before turning to her and hugging her. "You two will be Kahu Kai's power surgical team. This is fantastic news. I'm so happy. Shocked, but very happy."

Iolana was still in shock as her other colleagues got up to congratulate them. All she could do was smile as she tried not to telepathically explode Andrew's head for announcing their farce of a marriage at a staff meeting.

In one fell swoop her reputation for being a bit of an ice queen had come crashing down.

And she wasn't sure how she was going to survive being Andrew's wife, let alone his fiancée, because she was pretty sure, given the way she felt now, she was going to kill him.

Andrew winked at her as her father shook his hand again.

Yep. She was going to kill him.

CHAPTER TWO

ANDREW KNEW THAT he had poked the beast, but he wasn't in the least bit sorry about it. Lana had been testing him from the moment he'd walked into her office and she'd started making demands. When Jack had suggested that he ask his sister to participate in this marriage of convenience so he could get a green card he'd told Jack that he was nuts. One, because he was pretty sure Lana hated him. Two, they constantly butted heads. Three, he didn't know what was in it for her to agree to this; no one liked their brother that much. Four, her father was Chief of Surgery and he'd told Dr. Haole that he would take care of this green card issue himself and five, he was attracted to Lana.

So attracted to her.

In his eyes, Lana was not the right choice.

Only Jack had been damn insistent.

And Andrew was never one to look a gift horse in the mouth.

You're setting yourself up for a fall again.

He ignored that niggling thought. Whatever came of it came. He deserved whatever he had, good or bad. Even if it meant tempting his willpower in marrying, in name only, an attractive, fiery and passionate woman. Lana was tempting, but Andrew had willpower.

Are you sure?

From the moment he'd met her two years ago he had been enraptured by her. Her long black hair, dark eyes that sparkled in the waning sunlight and luscious lips that he desperately wanted to kiss. She had been standing on the beach at sunset in a wetsuit, holding a board and staring out over the ocean intensely. The way he used to stare at the waves after he surfed.

The way he longingly looked at the big waves because, since his accident, he had been unable to conquer the big waves. The groundswell waves that were generated by storms. The powerful waves that he wanted to conquer again.

Only he couldn't. And he had no one to blame but himself.

Now he was fake engaged to Lana and he was slightly concerned that she would conquer him in the end.

This is not real. You're not tying yourself down.

A real marriage and kids was not something he ever wanted. Not after his disaster of a childhood. He was selfish like his father and it was that selfishness which had caused the accident that injured his shoulder and killed his little sister.

He didn't deserve happiness.

In a year he'd have his green card and this marriage would be over. He'd be free again.

And lonely.

"You're engaged?" Dr. Keaka Haole asked, interrupting Andrew's thoughts as he shut the door to the now empty conference room. "After what happened with David, I have to say I'm surprised, Iolana."

Lana's expression changed from one of daggers to slight anxiety as she bit her full, pink bottom lip.

"I know, but this isn't like David. This is real. Which is why I've kept it quiet."

Dr. Haole looked at him shrewdly. "You love my daughter?"

"Yes, sir," Andrew said confidently. "My apologies for not asking for your blessing, but things kind of happened fast. We fell in love and..."

Dr. Haole put up his hand to silence him and

Andrew knew better than to tick off Dr. Keaka Haole Sr. Keaka Haole Jr. might be somewhat of a jovial fellow, but Keaka Sr. was not a man you wanted to trifle with.

Andrew wasn't terrified of him; he admired him.

The man was one of the best orthopedic surgeons in America. Andrew only wished when his shoulder had shattered that it was Dr. Keaka Haole who had operated on him and not that hack in northern Ontario who had botched his shoulder and ended his career as a surfer. Of course he deserved what he'd got that night.

"I'm not upset. Far from it," Dr. Haole said, smiling, which was rare for him.

"You're not?" Lana asked. Andrew couldn't help but hear the shock in her voice and it was the same sense of shock that he was experiencing.

"Of course not. Dr. Tremblay is an excellent physician and an asset to this hospital. You couldn't do any better, Iolana. As long as it's real. I won't have a repeat of what happened before."

"Why, thank you, Dr. Haole. Coming from you that means so much." Andrew tried to turn the conversation. He knew what had happened with

David and Lana. Even if it was before his time. Everyone knew about it.

David didn't deserve her.

And you do?

Only Lana knew this marriage was fake. According to the hospital drums, she'd been in love with David.

Lana glared at him quickly. "Dad, but…"

"Now, Iolana, it's okay. Usually I don't like it when you act impulsively, but this is really fantastic news. I've been telling you for years to settle down and get married."

Andrew put his arm around Lana and pulled her closer, beaming. "Well, Dr. Haole, we wanted to keep our relationship private while we were dating. We are professionals, after all."

Lana shrugged out of his embrace when her father's back was turned and he winked at her. He hadn't been expecting such easy acceptance from Dr. Haole. Andrew was not the kind of guy who got easy acceptance and approval from parental figures.

And then it hit him. He was deceiving a man he really admired for selfish reasons.

"So when will the wedding be?" Dr. Haole asked.

"As soon as possible," Lana said. "Just something simple, probably at the city hall or the court house in front of a judge. We just…"

"We just want to get married," Andrew said, finishing off Lana's sentence.

"We can do a proper wedding in a week."

"Father, you don't have to spend the money," Lana protested.

"Nonsense. You're my only daughter and we're going to do this right. I'll have your stepmother arrange everything so that it won't interrupt your surgical schedule." Dr. Haole stood up. "I'll call her up now and give her the news."

"Thank you," Lana said, but Andrew could tell she was unhappy. Even as her father took her in his arms and hugged her.

"I am so happy you have finally decided to settle down, Iolana. It means so much to me." Then Dr. Haole shook his hand.

"Thank you, Dr. Haole," Andrew managed to say, but he felt uneasy about the idea of a big wedding. Even though a big wedding would convince Immigration that it wasn't a fake wedding.

Only it is.

"Well, I have rounds to make," Lana said. "I'll talk to you later, Dad."

Andrew nodded and followed Lana out of the conference room. She didn't say anything as she walked quickly back to her office, but she didn't slam the door in his face either. She allowed him to come into her office and he shut the door.

"Well, you wanted a public proposal. Sorry I didn't get down on one knee." It was a half-hearted apology.

"That's not how I wanted it to happen." She was flustered. He'd never seen her like this and he felt bad because it was his fault it had been announced like that.

"I know, you mentioned one knee and a ring..."

She glared at him. "I would've preferred anything over that!"

"Why? It went well. You were nervous about telling your father. Jack was nervous over the idea of your father finding out. Now he knows and he seems quite thrilled with it."

She sighed. "Surprisingly. That actually caught me off guard, but then he's been harping on at me for the last five years to get married."

"Did you want to plan it?" Andrew asked.

"No," she snapped. "My stepmother will do a fine job. I really didn't want this in the first place!"

"I know."

"If you wanted to stay here you should've contacted an Immigration lawyer and done the right thing from the beginning, then we wouldn't be in this mess."

"I know," Andrew agreed. "Time slipped away from me. I was training the team and your brother. I kept putting it off…"

"Excuses," she raged. Then she sat down in her office chair. "You're a good doctor, but you are so disorganized."

"Office work is not my forte." His shoulder started to burn and he winced.

"I'll say," she groused and then looked at him as he rolled his shoulder. "What's wrong?"

"Just a twinge. Nothing more."

"Your shoulder hurts?"

"Nothing," he snapped as the pain hit him. "Look, I'd better go."

Lana got up and stepped in front of him. "I'm an orthopedic surgeon. I can take a look at your shoulder."

"I'm a surgeon too," he said. Although he didn't practice any more. He kept to the physical therapy side of sports medicine. Since his right shoulder repair had been botched the strength in his arm and hand came and went.

He wouldn't risk a patient's life on uncertainty.

"Let me look."

He sighed. "Anything to get my shirt off, eh?"

"Fine," she said through gritted teeth. "Be in pain."

"It's just a pulled muscle."

Liar.

He could've had Dr. Haole fix it, but again, he hadn't got around to it. Training Jack to make the World Surfing Championship was all that mattered. He didn't have the time to go under the knife, recover and then go through physical therapy.

He didn't have a year or more to waste.

What was done was done. It was a good reminder.

Besides, he didn't want Lana touching him. If she touched him he knew it would test his control. Since he'd first laid eyes on her he'd thought about her in a way he shouldn't.

This had to be an uncomplicated marriage.

He had to keep his hands to himself, as much as he didn't want to.

"Fine," she snapped.

"I have rounds to make."

She nodded, avoiding eye contact. "Me too."

"I guess I'll see you at this farce of a wedding in a week."

"I think before then. You want people to believe we're in love and you just announced it to the whole hospital that we're getting married."

"Not the whole hospital."

"You blabbed it to all the heads and chief residents that were in that meeting. You might as well have told everyone." Then she smiled a sad smile. "Word gets around fast here."

He chuckled. "You may be right on that one. So, would you like to go on a date tonight?"

"A date?"

"Yeah, we might as well have one, seeing how we're getting married and everything."

"Okay. That sounds…" She was cut off when her phone started ringing. "Dr. Haole speaking. Yes? How far out? Okay, I'll be down there in five."

"What was that?" Andrew asked.

"The emergency room. Incoming trauma; they need an orthopedic surgeon and I'm on call. I forgot. We'll have to do that date another night."

"I'll meet you down in the ER. I'll lend you a hand."

"You've never done an ER rotation since you got here," she said, astounded. "What about training?"

"The training can wait tonight. Jack will understand." Jack probably wouldn't, but Andrew didn't care. He wanted to be in that ER tonight. Show a united front to their upcoming wedding so it was believable.

He might not have surgical privileges, but he was still a doctor.

He could still help when it came to trauma.

CHAPTER THREE

LANA RETREATED TO the quiet calm of the operating room to repair a broken femur. She stood by, waiting as the trauma surgeon worked on stopping the blood flow in the major artery. She was just glad it wasn't David because he'd ply her with questions about Andrew.

Poor, pathetic, heartbroken Lana couldn't move on from him.

And she remembered how many times David and she had worked in the OR together. He'd been a fellow when she was a fourth year resident. She should've known—that was a red flag when he'd paid attention to her—but she'd craved the attention. The love and affection she'd never had.

Yeah, and look where that got you.

She shook her head and focused on the surgery. Once the rate of blood loss was managed she could go in and repair the femur. Piecing one of the strongest bones in the body back together.

As she waited she glanced up into the gallery, where residents were waiting to observe the surgery, and she noticed Andrew standing, watching. His arms were crossed and he looked pensive as he stared down into the OR.

Their eyes met and a small smile played across his face and she felt warmth flood her cheeks, but she was thankful that the surgical mask covered her face. She was still in shock and slightly angry that her father was so happy about the marriage.

Of course he didn't know it was a marriage of convenience, but after David she'd thought he wouldn't be so happy. And she was annoyed that her father was elated that she was finally taking his advice to settle down, implying that her life was worthless because she wasn't married or involved with anyone.

It wasn't that she repelled love. She'd been blinded by it. Hurt by it. So now her career was her first love. It never let her down.

After David she'd sworn to herself that she was going to get married for only the truest, deepest love. Her parents had married because they'd had to and they'd never been happy, which was why they were divorced.

And the moment her mother had been free from her father, she'd left.

Lana hadn't seen her mother since the day she'd graduated from medical school. And she doubted that she would see her at her wedding.

No doubt her mother wouldn't approve of her marriage to Andrew.

It's not real and you're not pregnant.

"Dr. Haole, we're ready for you now," the scrub nurse said.

"Thank you, Vickie." Lana took her place next to the trauma surgeon, Dr. Aeolia, who had been working on controlling the blood loss from the shattered femur.

"I hear congratulations are in order," Dr. Aeolia said as she began to formulate her game plan for repairing the femur in her head.

"Pardon?" Lana asked, not really listening to what Dr. Aeolia had to say.

"Your engagement. I was in the conference room when Dr. Tremblay announced it."

Oh, God.

This was exactly the kind of thing she wished she could avoid. She didn't like to be singled out, to have the attention drawn to her and as the words slipped out of Dr. Aeolia's mouth she could feel the gaze from all of those in the operating room fixed on her. Just like when David had dumped her. Humiliating her.

"How can you possibly think I love you? You have no spine. No fire and you're not as brilliant as your father thinks you are. This was purely a business move. I thought you knew that. I thought you knew that it would benefit us both!"

Lana shook David's cruel words from her head.

"Right," Lana said. "Thank you. Vickie, can you bring me my surgical tray?"

Vickie had been an orthopedic scrub nurse for years. She was her father's scrub nurse and knew exactly what surgical screws and plates would be needed to fix a broken femur.

"You don't sound happy about it," Dr. Aeolia said and Lana could sense the censure in her voice. Or maybe it wasn't censure, but jealousy.

She knew Dr. Aeolia lusted after Andrew, like most women did. Andrew was a playboy. A love 'em and leave 'em reputation that probably would hurt their story if they didn't play their cards right.

"I am, but right now I'm focused on fixing this patient's femur. Perhaps later we can discuss wedding arrangements, but not now." Lana's voice rose and as she glanced up into the gallery she could see Andrew grinning at her, giving her a subtle nod.

"Fine," Dr. Aeolia said with annoyance. "Since my job is making sure the patient is stabilized and will survive, I guess I can let you continue on with picking up the pieces. You're quite good at that, if I recall."

It was a jab that was laced with sarcasm, which Lana didn't care much for, but was used to. As the daughter of the Chief of Surgery she was used to people treating her like this. She knew very well that they all thought she was a spoiled princess. That she was Daddy's girl and got preferential treatment because of it.

When that was far from the truth.

She was not a princess. Everything she'd earned she'd worked hard for.

"You're right, Dr. Aeolia, your job here is done. Thank you; kindly leave my OR. I have it from here."

Dr. Aeolia glared at her over the surgical mask and Lana shook her head in annoyance as she continued to work on stabilizing and preparing the femur.

She didn't have many friends in this hospital

and she tried to tell herself she didn't care, but she did. She was alone.

It was why she was known as a bit of an ice queen.

And she was fine with letting them think that. It was easier on her heart.

Lana knew who she really was.

Do you?

And as she glanced back up at the gallery she saw that Andrew had left. She breathed an inward sigh of relief and continued on her repair of the femur. She was glad he was gone because he was a distraction and that was the last thing she needed in her life.

Just go home. You don't need to wait for her.

Only Andrew was waiting for her in the main lobby. Just like a dutiful fiancé would. He had been so impressed with the way Lana had handled herself in the operating room under the scrutiny of Dr. Aeolia, who was a big gossip and who had been hitting on him since he'd first arrived, but he had no interest in her.

Now, he wanted to show the rest of them this was for real.

Except it's not.

He rolled his stiff shoulder and then got up from where he'd been sitting in an uncomfortable lobby chair and began to pace as he waited for Lana. Her surgery on the femur had been done hours ago and it was the middle of the night, but there was a diner where a twenty-four-hour breakfast was served. He could at least treat her to some kind of meal and then maybe they could talk.

Get their stories straight so they could present a united front.

As he rolled his stiff shoulder he saw her on the breezeway, in her street clothes, walking down he steps to the main lobby. She looked tired, but that still didn't detract from her grace and beauty. The Ice Queen of Oahu.

Which was an unfair name, because even though she tried to put up an appearance of being frosty he knew there was a warmth about her when she dealt with patients and her younger brother Jack. A caring side, even if she didn't want to admit to it.

She looked up at him, her dark eyes widening in shock. "Dr.…Andrew, what're you doing here still? It's three in the morning!"

"I went home and had a sleep, but thought

I would come back and take you out for a bite to eat."

"It's three in the morning," she repeated.

"I know, but the Kahuna Café on the north shore is open twenty-four hours and their specialty is breakfast."

She wrinkled her nose. "That place looks like a dive."

"It's not a dive. Are you telling me that you've never been to the Kahuna Café?"

"No, it was never somewhere my parents took us."

"Jack likes it," Andrew teased.

Lana smirked. "Jack would eat his own hat if it was deep fried."

Andrew chuckled. "True. Come on, what do you say? Come have some early breakfast with me and then I'll take you home."

"Fine."

"Hey, it's not a punishment, you know," he teased.

"What?" she asked as she fell into step beside him.

"Going out to eat breakfast with me. I'm not a monster."

A smile played on her lips. "I never said you

were. Perhaps I'm the monster. I am considered a bit of a…"

"You don't have to say it. I've heard it," he teased. "What I'm saying is that appearances can be deceiving and you, of all people, should understand that."

"Sorry," she said.

"No problem, sweetie."

Lana wrinkled her nose. "Ugh, don't call me sweetie."

"Pookie?"

"Nope."

"Polkaroo?"

"What?" she asked, confused.

He chuckled at his subtle Canadian joke that he knew that she would never get. "Never mind. You don't want an endearment nickname?"

"No, thank you. Just Lana is fine by me."

"Okay." Then he picked up her hand and she snatched it back as if he were on fire.

"What're you doing?" she said under her breath.

"There are people watching," he whispered.

Lana took his hand grudgingly. He'd never really held a woman's hand before. He wasn't a touchy-feely guy—well, he was never one for public displays of affection, because public displays of affection meant something more. It meant permanence, romance and he wasn't a permanent sort of guy. But holding Lana's hand felt right.

And that made him nervous.

It's because people are watching. It doesn't mean anything.

And then tension settled between them. It was completely awkward and no one in their right mind would believe that they were in love and the marriage was for real unless he eased this tension.

"How did surgery go?" He winced because it was a dumb question. He knew how it had gone. Lana was a brilliant surgeon and he knew the patient had pulled through.

There were good odds he was going to make it, although there would be a long road to recovery. Andrew knew firsthand the pain of physical therapy.

"It went well," Lana said and he could tell by her tone she thought it was a weird question too.

He let go of her hand and opened the passenger side door to his car. When he shut the door he rolled his eyes. Annoyed with himself.

Why had he thought this was going to be easy? When had anything in life been simple?

Never.

Lana and Jack might be siblings but they were complete opposites. Jack was so warm and open. Lana was closed off and cold. He had heard the term *ice queen* bounced around about Lana and he got it. There was a social awkwardness there at the very least.

Yet, in her office, talking about the terms of their engagement she'd been warm and funny. Feisty even. And he was sure that was the real her, but she was suppressing it and he didn't know why.

The drive to the Kahuna Café was laced with quiet tension, but when they pulled into the parking lot a smile crept across her face.

"That's a lot of Tiki masks," she teased.

Andrew chuckled. The place was a bit kitschy and totally catered to tourists, but he loved it. The food was simple and good. It reminded him of the small diner outside the east gate of Algonquin Park in the town he'd grown up in.

He hadn't been back to north-eastern Ontario in several years. There was nothing for him there, but there were moments when he missed things and the Kahuna Café, a world away from Whitney, Ontario, brought back just a piece of home.

And when he thought about home, he thought about his sister, Meghan, which made his heart hurt. God, he missed her. And it had been a while since he'd really thought about her.

"You killed her! It's all your fault, Andrew! You killed your sister. How could you be so reckless?"

"This is why I've never been here," Lana teased, interrupting the memory of that horrible night from his mind.

"Why? Because of the Tiki masks?"

"My dad would never come here."

"Well, your dad isn't here, so what do you think?" he asked.

She bit her lip in concentration as she slid out of the car. "I'll let you know after I taste the food."

Andrew grinned and opened the door to the café and they walked in to an almost empty diner. There were a few people, farmers and tourists alike, but the diner was mostly empty. Another reason he liked this place so much.

They slid into a booth and the waitress brought them coffee.

"Mahalo." Lana thanked the waitress, who nodded. "So what would you like to talk about?"

"Well, our wedding for starters," he said.

"I don't think we really have to discuss much with respect to plans."

"Oh?" Andrew asked.

"My stepmother loves to plan parties. She'll take care of everything. She is the top wedding planner in Waikiki."

"How over-the-top is this thing going to be?" he asked suddenly, dreading a crazy fiasco.

Lana grinned. "Over. Way over."

Andrew groaned. "Well, at least it will be convincing."

"They don't know that..." Lana trailed off. "It's real as far as they're concerned."

"True. Okay, but what about after?" It was hard for him to talk about after. He never had relationships, just flings. There was never an after. It was weird to talk about after when this wasn't a real marriage.

"After?" she asked.

"Living arrangements. I remember that you suggested my moving in with you, but we didn't actually decide, did we?"

Lana tried not to choke on her coffee.

Living arrangements?

The waitress came over. “Are you ready to order?”

“Just some toast,” Lana said because she didn’t really feel like eating all of a sudden.

“Nothing for me,” Andrew said. “Coffee is fine.”

The waitress left and Lana found the words that were struggling to come out. The reality of ‘married’ life was becoming all too clear.

“To sell our marriage to Immigration, we will have to live under the same roof. For at least a year.”

He sounded just as freaked out as she was.

Andrew was right, but the thought of sharing her home with him, a man who simultaneously drove her bonkers and who she was wildly attracted to, was scary.

How could she live under the same roof as him?

“It does make sense if you move in with me.” She looked reluctant, though. “I mean, I don’t even know exactly where your apartment is.”

He grinned, that sly mischievous grin which caused a dimple to appear in his cheek.

Dang, his teeth were so white and perfect.

“That’s pretty bad that you don’t even know where your husband lives.”

Heat bloomed in her cheeks. "You're not my husband yet."

Andrew laughed, and she liked it when he laughed. She wasn't used to this. Usually he was so serious around her. She'd watched him be charming to others from afar.

But he was never this way with her.

She liked this.

Don't get carried away. This isn't real.

"So, your place, then?" he asked.

"Well, my house is near the hospital and the beach. I have three bedrooms and a pool."

Andrew raised his eyebrows in surprise. "Really?"

"Now who doesn't know where the other lives?" she teased.

"Since I'm in a bachelor apartment I guess I'll move in with you."

"Don't be so dramatic," she said. "I'm sure it's not a hardship."

"Oh, but it is."

"Yeah, well, I'm not moving in with you." The waitress set down the toast and poured more coffee.

"My bachelor pad is nice. Sparse but nice."

"Sparse but nice?" she teased. "I don't do

sparse. I like neat and organized, but sparse? That's just sad."

They laughed together and she couldn't remember the last time she'd laughed like this. She'd never laughed like this with David. Not even with her father.

"Don't be so silly, Iolana. Act your age. Be respectable."

"I like this," he said.

"What, toast and coffee at three in the morning?" she asked.

"Yeah, but also this side of you. Why do you keep this side of you locked away?"

Lana felt her cheeks heat again and she cleared her throat to regain composure. She couldn't let him in. "I don't know what you're talking about."

He frowned. "Fine."

She felt bad for throwing up a wall, but it was her best form of defense. And now the toast was like gravel in her mouth; she could barely choke it down.

"So when do you want to move in?" she asked, changing the subject.

"How about after we're married? I think your dad is a traditional sort of guy."

"That's true. He is." She sighed. "I'm exhausted. I really should get home and get some rest."

Andrew nodded. "I'll take you home."

"Just back to the hospital is fine. I have to get my car."

"Right."

They both threw down some money for breakfast and then walked out to his car. Lana was nervous, as if she were on a date—one that ended badly.

Only she wasn't on a date. This wasn't real. They had just been formulating an intricate ruse.

And she had to keep telling herself that.

CHAPTER FOUR

LANA MANAGED TO avoid Andrew for the rest of the week. Even though the wedding was creeping up fast, she was actively avoiding him. He'd made her feel things at the Kahuna Café that she wasn't comfortable with. Things that she'd hidden for so long because it was expected of her. Her father had certain expectations, but there was a part of her deep down that was like her mother.

And it was that side she hid because it was too painful for her father.

When her mother had left, shortly after Jack was born, she'd assumed the mantle of mother.

And since she wanted Jack and her father happy, she'd buried the feelings of grief, anger and loss well. Only one other person had got through her icy shell and that had been David.

David had made her feel things she'd never thought possible and look how well that had turned out.

Then there was the constant butting of heads

between her brother and father. So Lana had learned to adapt to smooth things over between the two of them. She was the mediator and the peacekeeper. So, to make sure everyone was happy she'd do almost anything.

Even wear a wedding dress that slightly horrified her.

"It's so dreamy," Sophie, her stepmother, gushed, running her manicured hand over the fabric as if it were one of the fluffy poodles she showed. "Isn't it, Lana?"

You expect me to wear that?

Only she didn't say that.

Keep the peace. Keep the peace.

"Sure."

There wasn't anything inherently wrong with the dress. It was just…she wasn't used to dresses. They weren't something she was used to wearing. Especially one that was lace-covered, form-fitting, backless, ivory-colored and scattered with pearls.

That wasn't her idea of nice clothing.

She'd missed her prom because her father had been at a medical conference and someone had to watch Jack. Maybe she was the only girl who didn't dream of being Cinderella.

Give her scrubs, slacks or a wetsuit any day.

Oh, come on. You dreamt of wedding dresses when you were with David.

And she hated herself for letting that thought in.

Sophie frowned. “You hate it, don’t you?”

“No, no,” Lana apologized quickly. “It’s just overwhelming. I hadn’t planned on…”

Getting married after David had crushed her heart. Having a wedding. Getting married to Andrew ever.

“I hadn’t planned on a wedding.” Which wasn’t a lie. “We just wanted to go down to City Hall. Do it quietly.”

Sophie smiled. “Which is why I’m planning it. I am the best wedding planner on the island.”

“I know.” Lana smiled. Sophie wasn’t her mother, but she was the closest she’d had to one for the last fifteen years. Sophie had stepped in when Lana had gone to school in California. And she sometimes couldn’t help but wonder if her father had remarried just so there was someone to take care of Jack when she was away. But then that made her wonder: had he only let her go because she was following in his footsteps?

Don’t think like that. Dad loves Sophie and so

do you. It killed Lana to be lying to her on so many levels. “I do love it. Truly.”

“I knew it.” Sophie clapped her hands and put the dress back in its garment bag before swinging around with another garment bag. “I have your gala dress ready too.”

Lana groaned inwardly. Right. The gala fundraiser was the night before her wedding. Two fancy dresses in the span of twenty-four hours. This would be brutal.

Lana braced herself, but as Sophie pulled out a royal blue, long ball gown, also backless and covered in lace, she relaxed because it was completely stunning. This dress she really did love. Royal blue was one of her favorite colors.

“I can see by the way your eyes lit up you like this one more,” Sophie teased.

“I do.” Lana touched the dress. “Can’t I get married in this?”

“No, no. It’s ivory for a sunset wedding on the beach. It’s traditional and your father wants traditional.” Sophie took the gala dress and zipped it back up in its garment bag before handing it over to Lana. “I’ll keep the wedding gown at the house, but since the gala is tomorrow night I’ll leave this dress with you.”

"Thanks, Sophie." And she truly did mean it. She would be lost without her stepmother. This whole thing was so out of her league.

Sophie kissed her cheek. "Any time."

Lana walked her out and then once the door was shut she sank down in her office chair, trying not to let this farce of a marriage overwhelm her.

Too late.

There was a knock and, before she could say *Don't come in*, Andrew came barging in. She startled at seeing him. In the past week she'd seen him in the halls when he wasn't training Jack, but she'd kept her nose down in whatever she was doing to ignore him and avoid him. In her office there was no escaping him. She was trapped. He took one look at her and he frowned.

"What's wrong?" he asked as he shut the door.

"Nothing."

"You looked like you were about explode." He crossed his arms, his eyes narrowing as he assessed her.

Because I am.

"I'm fine. Just busy. What can I do for you?"

"I have a patient I need a consult on."

She was taken aback. Andrew always went to her father when it came to consults. Never her.

Which was a slap in the face. Her father might be Chief of Surgery but she was Head of Ortho. Her father was so busy with administration he didn't clock as many hours in the operating room any more. She was clocking more hours, but other surgeons rarely sought her opinion. "Is my father unavailable?"

"No, but I'd like your opinion."

"Why?" she asked cautiously.

"Why not?" He gave her a questioning look. "Why are you so uncomfortable about this?"

"I'm not uncomfortable."

His eyes narrowed. "You totally are."

"You've never wanted my opinion on your patients before… You always went to my father."

"I never saw you operate before and when I observed you for that femur repair and how you did that surgery I was impressed."

"How gracious of you to notice."

Andrew rolled his eyes. "Fine. I want your opinion because it would look good. You've been distant this past week; people are noticing. Is that what you wanted to hear?"

"Fine." She grinned sweetly at him. "I just wanted the truth."

"You're so infuriating! I told you the truth. You're an impressive surgeon."

"If I'm so impressive why don't you let me look at your shoulder? You seem to roll it or wince a lot. Does it bother you?"

That caught him off guard. Instead of annoyance, a cold firmness set in his jaw. The twinkle went out of his eyes. "I'm fine. A little tension, nothing a good massage won't fix."

"I think..."

"I said I'm fine," he snapped and she knew that she was pushing him too far.

"Let's go see your patient," she said, exasperated.

Andrew nodded, but wouldn't look her in the eye. She felt bad for pushing him, but she couldn't help but wonder why he was so sensitive about his shoulder. It could be a simple fix if it was injured. That was if it was more than a little tension. It might not even require surgery but physiotherapy, but it was as if he'd given up on it.

Can't you relate?

Hadn't she given up on a lot of things? Things that she really didn't want to discuss because they too were a sore spot. It wasn't any of her business, because she didn't want people prying into her life. After David she was tired of being under the microscope and it was apparent by the way Andrew threw up a wall so fast that he didn't want her to pry into his life either.

"So what seems to be the problem?" Lana asked as they walked side by side down the hall. She wanted to change the subject. "What do you need me to look at?"

"The patient came in with what appeared to be a simple shoulder dislocation, but the X-rays are unclear. I think he'll need surgery because if I try to pop that shoulder back into the socket I think it's just going to pop right back out or it'll puncture his lung if I try to put it back into place manually."

"Did he say how he did it?"

"Golfing," Andrew remarked. "He's a tourist. He's also French."

"Does he speak English?"

Andrew grinned and waggled his eyebrows playfully. "Well, he did until we gave him sedation. He's been saying a bunch of interesting things now."

Lana groaned. No wonder he hadn't asked her father to do this.

Andrew wanted to torture her. As soon as they entered the room the patient grinned at her.

"Monsieur, Je vous presenté mon collègue, le Dr Haole, voir votre bras."

The patient just grinned. *"Ah, quelle belle femme!"*

"What did he say?" Lana asked under her breath.

"He said what a beautiful woman."

"Clearly he's drugged up," she muttered as she pulled on a trauma gown and gloves so she could inspect the patient more closely.

"Why would you imply that?" Andrew asked, puzzled.

"Imply what?" she said, distracted.

"That the compliment really isn't a compliment because the patient is drugged up. You're very attractive, Lana, and, sedated or not, I believe he's speaking the truth. You are very beautiful."

Andrew's declaration made her heart skip a beat. Warmth flooded her cheeks.

"Lana, you're beautiful. Sexy. And we look good together. We'll be a power couple. Why do we need love? Isn't that enough?"

Hollow compliments. That's all David ever paid her.

Andrew was just a playboy. It was just probably part of the act of seduction.

She cleared her throat. "Get him to lift his arm, would you?"

Andrew didn't know why she'd brushed off their patient's compliment, as if only a sedated man would find her attractive. The notion was preposterous.

Lana was attractive.

Which was why the proposition of entering into this marriage of convenience with her was a scary thought indeed.

Only because he wasn't so sure being alone with her outside this hospital was a good idea. He wasn't sure he would be able to keep his hands off her.

And he respected her as a colleague too much to ruin her life, but he was too deep into this charade to change course now.

She was the most beautiful woman he'd ever seen, which was why being around her was so dangerous for him. When he was around her it was an internal struggle not to pull her into his arms and kiss her, but she was completely off limits.

Of course that complicated matters, as they were getting married in a couple of days.

He just wasn't a relationship kind of guy and he wouldn't hurt Lana. She deserved more than he could offer her.

Which was nothing. He could offer her nothing.

What she was doing for him—there was no way that he could ever make up for that. Except keep his distance, no matter how much he wanted to bridge the gap between the two of them. His blood heated just thinking about taking her in his arms, running his fingers through her long, silky black hair and kissing those soft pink lips.

A scream shook him out of his dangerous thoughts.

"*Zut, zut, zut...*" the patient slurred through sedation.

"*Donc désolé, monsieur. Il sera bientôt fini,*" he quickly apologized as the man writhed in pain.

Lana winced as she held the man down to stop him from injuring himself more. "I take it that's not a pleasant word."

"See, you understand French perfectly," Andrew teased as he tried to calm their patient down with a shot of morphine.

"The examination's all done," Lana said.

Andrew translated and the patient visibly relaxed. "Well, what's the verdict?"

Although he knew. The way the man had screamed. This wasn't just a simple run-of-the-mill dislocated shoulder. This was something more.

"He's going to need surgery," she said as she peeled off her gloves. "I'll go prep the OR and if you could run all the pre-operative labs and make sure his next of kin is notified that would be helpful."

"Can do," Andrew said quickly. "Is there anything else I can do to assist you, Lana?"

"You could come into the OR with me. You have surgical training. You could advise me."

It wasn't an unreasonable request. This man was his patient, he did have a surgical license, but he didn't practice here for a very good reason. He didn't trust himself to hold a scalpel. And he didn't trust his reaction walking into that OR. The memories of what had happened to him, his crushed hopes and dreams, all because of a foolish mistake which had cost him his dreams of becoming a world champion surfer. Cost his sister her life.

And the OR, a place that he used to love, was now a place he loathed.

"I don't have surgical privileges at this hospital," he said and he hoped that would be enough to deter her. It was usually enough to deter other surgeons who asked him questions that he wasn't comfortable answering.

"I'm not asking you to assist, but this is your patient too."

She was right, but he just couldn't go in there. Even though he missed it. Even though he had been a damn good surgeon before his shoulder had been destroyed. When his hands could grip properly.

When his back wasn't so marred with scars from a surgery that had been botched.

The OR had been a place he loved. A chance to do the work he loved. It was exciting and challenging yet it grounded him. Almost as much as surfing. There was a thrill in the operating room, just like when he was on a board and shredding the nar.

And now he couldn't do either.

At least he could coach Jack in surfing. At least he could be there as Jack's sports medicine physician and get him to the world championships.

Provided Lana and he were able to pull off this farce of a marriage.

"I'm sorry, Lana, but I can't. I have other patients to see. I am the orthopedic doctor on call tonight. I diagnose them, you operate on them."

She looked as if she was going to say more, but instead she nodded. "Okay, well, just make sure his labs get done and his family is notified. I'll send a resident to come fetch him when it's time to go to the OR. Start him on some antibiotics as well."

I know.

"Will do."

Lana nodded and left him. Andrew gripped the clipboard, his one good arm holding it tightly but his other arm shaking because it was weak and for that he hated himself a bit.

The surgery was almost textbook. Several times Lana looked up in the gallery to see if Andrew was up there, like he had been before, but he wasn't. He was so afraid of the operating room.

What had happened?

She knew he had been a surgeon up in Canada. And she knew that he'd been a successful one.

A sought-after surgeon who was innovative and ground-breaking. So why had he given it up?

Her father would grant Andrew surgical privileges in a heartbeat if Andrew gave any indication that he wanted to get back into the operating room. It actually made her a bit nervous when he did watch her.

Andrew had developed a bone flap method known as the Tremblay that was being used widely in Canada and across most states. Yet he had never offered to show anyone that technique. She'd always thought he just wanted to keep it to himself for job security, but now that he kept refusing to go into the operating room, and didn't ask for surgical privileges, she couldn't help but wonder more.

And she wondered if it had something to do with the shoulder and arm that seemed to grieve him the most.

Muscle tension, my ass!

Once she'd made sure their tourist patient was comfortable, out of the recovery room and in the care of a nurse that spoke French fluently she was able to finally go home for the night.

As she was gathering up her stuff, including

the garment bag which held the dress for the gala tomorrow night, she passed by the Attending lounge. Drawn by the flicker of the television screen, she peered in the door.

Andrew was in there; he was leaned over, staring intently at the screen. He was watching a surfing semifinal, but she didn't know from what year and it was too far away to make out who the surfer was.

When the surfer, riding on an enormous wave, fell off the board she winced.

That had to be a hard fall.

Andrew flicked off the television and then leaned over, his face buried in his hands, but only for a moment as he dragged his hands through his hair. She could see him mouthing curse words through the window.

She backed away from the Attending lounge because she didn't want him to see her standing there, staring at him.

It was bad enough that when he was around she had a hard time focusing. He made her hot under the collar. He was dangerous to be around.

She'd had her heart broken by a cad before.

Ever since then she'd learned not to allow herself near men like Andrew Tremblay.

Except you're marrying him in forty-eight hours.

Lana shook her head. She had to get out of here.

Tomorrow was her day off, thankfully. All she wanted to do was get home, shower and get a good night's sleep. And tomorrow morning she'd hit the beach with her board and just forget everything for a while.

It had been a long time since she'd surfed. Usually she was too busy, but tomorrow was a good time to burn off some steam. Some frustration and some sexual tension that she was experiencing lately since she had to deal with Andrew Tremblay on a regular basis.

She only hoped the weather cooperated or she might do something she'd regret the next morning.

And the thing was, she was going to have to stay married to her possible regret for a year.

There would be no escape. No easy out if she decided to walk down that uneasy path. She was too far down the rabbit hole now; there were too many people she'd disappoint if she backed out of the marriage of convenience now.

She was just going to do everything in her power not to fall prey to Andrew Tremblay's charms.

Easier said than done.

CHAPTER FIVE

TODAY WAS A perfect day to surf. The sea, the sun and the breeze. The water was dappled like diamonds in the brilliant sun.

The only shadow on the day and his plans was his bum shoulder and the fact tonight he had to attend a gala with Lana.

Andrew cursed himself inwardly for giving Jack the day off from training when he saw how ripe the waves were. He'd thought he was doing himself a favor by giving Jack the day off so he could just spend the day collecting his thoughts.

Last night, after he'd walked away from yet another surgery, he'd gone and watched surfing on television. Something he hadn't done well since his accident. It was a video of his days before the accident. When he had been carefree and Meghan had been alive. From the days when he was still a surgeon and not the half man he'd become. When the whole world had been his for the taking. Now he deserved none of it.

He didn't know what had compelled him to watch it.

You're sick and twisted. That's why.

Now, he was torturing himself further by walking on the beach in the early morning and watching choice waves roll in from the Pacific. This was not going to calm him down in time to escort Lana to the gala tonight. In fact it made him more agitated and he wanted to call it all off, but he couldn't. He was in too deep.

The gala would be their first real test since announcing their engagement, proving to the world that they were a real couple.

He didn't know what he was thinking, coming to the beach. As he longingly watched the waves, his hands jammed into his pockets, he spotted a surfer paddling to the shore and then hefting her bright turquoise board out of the water.

Oh, holy heck.

He'd come down here to collect his thoughts and prepare himself for the charade tonight. To steel himself against doing something crazy impulsive with Lana. And now here she was, coming out of the waves, just like the first time he'd seen her.

The short sleeve wetsuit clinging to her curves,

her black hair slicked back from the water. The ocean glistening off her exposed skin like diamonds. It took him back to that day a couple of years ago when he'd first seen her. When he was first enticed by her and then realized she was Jack's sister and therefore off limits.

Pull yourself together.

As if she knew that he was staring at her, Lana looked up, her dark eyes widening in surprise when she saw him.

"Andrew?"

There was no backing out and running the opposite way. He waved and walked over toward her, but keeping a safe distance so he wouldn't act impulsively.

"Good morning, Lana. A very nice day, isn't it?"

A very nice day, isn't it? You idiot.

What, was he in junior high again? At least his voice didn't crack this time.

"It is," she said and looked a bit surprised to see him. "I didn't expect to see you here. Jack said he had the morning off and was lounging around in my pool."

"That's what he does on his day off? I thought he'd at least go to the gym."

Lana snorted. "With my brother you have to take him there yourself. He's easily distracted."

So am I at the moment. Only he didn't say that out loud. "I didn't expect to see you here, Lana."

"I have the day off too. I thought I would clear my head before tonight." She bent down and undid the strap around her ankle. With her quick movement, he swore he could smell the scent of coconut mixed in with the salt water.

It was intoxicating. It reminded him of summer, sand and surf and all the things he loved.

Get a hold of yourself.

"How were the waves?" he asked, feeling like a complete fool for the asinine conversation. He knew how the waves were. He could see them for himself.

"They were great," she sighed. "I wish I could spend all day out here, but I have to do some stuff to get ready for the gala tonight."

"Right, the gala."

"What time are you picking me up?" she asked.

"I'm picking you up?" he asked, confused.

She smirked at him. "Don't you think it would be a bit odd if my date and fiancé didn't pick me up and take me to the gala?"

"I assumed you were going with your father," he said.

"Usually, but this time wouldn't it make more sense to go with my fiancé?"

"Right." He scrubbed his hand over his face. "I'm not used to this."

"I can see that."

"I guess I'm just used to you accompanying your father."

"I told him that I would forgo the big limousine and ride with you. My fiancé. He seemed on board with it." There was a teasing glint in her eyes. He liked this Iolana. He liked her feisty, just like she had been when they'd first agreed to this marriage of convenience.

The subdued version made him want to shake her. Tell her that she was made of stronger stuff, but that was not his place. This was just a hint of the real Iolana and he didn't want to scare her away.

"I suppose you have a valid point," he conceded. "What time would you like me to pick you up?"

"I have to be there early." She bit that lip, that luscious full lip that he so wanted to bite too. "Seven? Is that good?"

"Seven is perfect, but I still don't know where you live. I guess I should know since I'm going to be moving into your place after we're married."

"Come on, I'll take you there." She picked up her board under one arm and headed off the beach. Andrew didn't see any cars nearby and then he realized she was heading for a set of wooden steps that wound their way through some foliage and up into a house that always reminded him of a treehouse.

He loved this house, but he'd never known who it belonged to. Until now.

"This is your place?" he asked, thrilled and shocked all at once. He'd pictured her living in some quaint little cottage. Neat and tidy. A treehouse was so unexpected. He'd never seen Lana as the free spirit type. The adventurer. He'd seen her as safe and reliable. Sensible. A treehouse was not sensible.

"Yes. My father comes from one of the richest families on the island. This was my grandmother's place until she died and she left it to me."

"I've always admired this place."

"It's a great place." Lana set her board down on a landing. She unlocked a rack that held many other boards.

"You want me to wipe it down?" Andrew asked; he wanted a closer look at some of her boards.

"I'll wipe it down later."

After she locked it up he followed her up the steps again, almost to the treetops as they headed out onto a wooden balcony that had a view of the sea, but was shaded from the hot sun by the thick growth of palms and ferns. Almost like a natural lanai.

"You have a pool up here?" Andrew asked, confused. They were off the ground, in the treetops almost, so he couldn't figure out where there would be a pool.

"Out front there's a small lap pool and a hot tub. The kitchen and living room are upstairs, the bedrooms are downstairs, where the pool and the main road is. It's sort of a bi-level house."

"I hope Jack is doing laps. He needs to build up his shoulder strength."

Lana snorted as she put a clip in her wet hair. "I highly doubt that Jack is doing laps. He's probably in the hot tub."

Before he could say anything else he realized she was unzipping her spring suit. His blood heated and he tried to avert his eyes as she peeled away the neoprene body suit to reveal a bikini underneath.

Lithe, bronze and curves in all the right places.

Don't look. Don't look.

So he started to stare up at the foliage and soon came to the realization the foliage sucked and he'd rather be looking at something more intoxicating.

"Are you okay?" she asked.

"I'm good, just checking out the view. Love the canopy you have here. Very natural."

Andrew heard her chuckle as if she knew he wasn't checking out the foliage.

"Come on, let's go see if Jack is doing what he's supposed to be doing and I can give you a quick tour of your new place."

He braved a look and saw that she'd thrown on a sundress over her bikini, but still he couldn't get that image out of his mind.

Why did he have to be so attracted to her? This was just supposed to be a sort of business arrangement.

"There's an extra bedroom up here. It's small, but I think it will work for you." Lana opened the door to a medium-sized bedroom that was off the living room. “It has its own bathroom and faces the ocean.”

Andrew peered around the room. There was a bed and dresser. The bathroom was small, but had a shower and as he wandered over to the window he was impressed by the view. It would do perfectly.

“This is great,” he said. “Thanks.”

“It’s no big deal. We have to live together. I’m not going to make you bunk out in the shed. As much as I’m tempted to.” Her dark eyes were sparkling at the dig.

Andrew chuckled at that. “I’ve lived in worse places. I’m sure your shed is fine.”

“It has spiders.”

“They don’t bug me.”

“That’s a pathetic pun,” she said drily.

“Do you hate insect puns?”

“Yes.”

“Do they bug you?”

“You’re crazy.” She rolled her eyes. “Come on, I’ll take you out to the pool.”

Andrew followed her and spied the kitchen and sunken living room that was open concept. It was well organized, modern, but definitely feminine.

There was a vase full of flowers and other little touches that were not in his home.

He housed the few books he had in a set of plastic milk crates and his futon mattress was raised off the floor by some wooden skids he'd found.

Andrew had the money to buy a nice place, to have nice things, but he preferred living that way. He liked to be able to pack up in a rucksack and leave. He liked that most of his life could fit in the trunk of his car.

Things just tied people down.

They were anchors and burdens. He didn't want any of it, but as he walked around Lana's place he felt a twinge of something that he hadn't felt in a long time. A sense of belonging and it frightened him.

He didn't deserve it. He didn't deserve happiness or a sense of security. Andrew often wondered why he'd gone on living when Meghan died. It might've been better in the long run if he'd died in that accident and she'd lived.

Their parents wouldn't have disowned her. She had so much potential.

The steps down from the main level led to the front door. There was another small living area that overlooked the front patio that was fenced by a cement wall and more greenery. Behind him were a couple of doors that he assumed led to where Lana slept.

She slid open the patio door to head out to the pool area. The lap pool was empty. "See, he's not doing laps. He's in the hot tub."

As Andrew's eyes adjusted to the light he saw at the far end, under another lanai, was Jack, head back, eyes closed and in the hot tub.

"You better be wearing shorts!" Lana called out.

Jack startled and Andrew waved at him. "Hey, Jack. I thought you'd be training, building up your arm strength?"

"You brought Andrew, Iolana?" Jack whined. "And I am wearing shorts. I've learned my lesson."

Andrew turned to Lana. "What did you do to him?"

She grinned. "Had a few girlfriends over. He had his headphones in, listening to music, so I hid his clothes. Made him streak across my yard. Gave everyone a good laugh."

He chuckled. "That's evil. Remind me not to get on your bad side."

"Too late." Then she laughed and he couldn't

help but laugh with her. "Though you're safe for now. As long as you don't annoy me too much."

"I can't promise that." He winked and she laughed again.

Jack wrapped a towel around himself and walked over. "I thought you were out surfing, Lana?"

"I was. I was gone for two hours." She shook her head. "You know, once I'm married you can't come here and mooch off me anymore."

Jack rolled his eyes. "Where else am I going to go?"

"You could use my place," Andrew offered. "Since I'll be moving in here."

"No, thanks, your place should be condemned. No offense, Doc."

Andrew grinned smugly. "Why don't you do some laps for me? And I'm going to sit here and watch."

Jack groaned. "Fine."

"I'll leave you two to that. I'm going to take a shower and wash the salt water off." Lana went back inside and disappeared into the far room, shutting the door. Andrew tried not to think of her in that room, naked and having a shower. Or the fact he wanted to join her.

"You looking forward to the gala tonight?" Jack asked, interrupting his thoughts.

"No. I don't have a tuxedo."

"You can borrow mine. After I do my laps I'll go get it at Dad's place. It should fit you."

"Thanks."

"No problem." Jack dropped his towel and slipped into the pool. "How many?"

"Fifty," Andrew said, taking a seat on one of the deckchairs. He turned back and looked toward the house. He didn't really want to go to this gala; he usually avoided them, but he wanted to look good for Lana, who was the Chief of Surgery's daughter.

He wanted the world to think he deserved her, when that was the furthest thing from the truth.

Lana loved the dress, but she was so uncomfortable. Usually for the big hospital gala she wore a little black number with pearls and flats—very understated—and she went with her father and stepmother.

Even when she was with David it hadn't felt like anything romantic. It had been more like a business dinner rather than a date.

"Really, that's what you're wearing?"

"What? I like it."

"Don't you even want to try? You can be such an embarrassment sometimes. Thank goodness you're pretty."

Lana shook away that thought. Angry that she'd let David into her life and let him walk over her, blind to his lack of emotion. Everyone else had seen it but her, which made her all the more pathetic.

Stop thinking like that.

She shook those thoughts out of her head. She had to clear her mind because Andrew was coming over soon to take her to the gala.

It was the first time in a long time she'd been on a date. Period. After David it was hard to trust men and hard to date when she had an orthopedic practice to run.

Men were interested in her looks, her money, but once they discovered she had a brain and that her first love was her career then they realized that money and good looks weren't enough. She'd been referred to as frigid and cold.

That suited her just fine.

Lana had always lived by the mantra that she didn't need a man to make her happy. Which was why it disappointed her that her father was so happy about this marriage. He'd never viewed her career with as much enthusiasm as he was showing in her marriage to Andrew. He'd told her that he was proud of her for growing up and settling down.

Why did that have to include marriage?

It frustrated her and also upset her that her father thought so little of her. That he pinned a happy future for her on getting married. He'd done the same when she'd been with David and now he was doing it again.

It's not real. It's not real.

And Lana had to keep reminding herself of that fact. This was temporary. It was only for a year. She knew it would crush her father when she came to him this time next year and told him the marriage was over.

Just the thought of his reaction made her dread it, because he would be looking on her with sympathy and she didn't need that. She would just have to take it in her stride. It would cause a bigger scandal for her father and the hospital if she backed out of it now and Andrew was deported back to Canada.

Her doorbell chimed and she took a deep breath. With one final check in the mirror, she ran her hands down over the form-fitting royal blue dress and headed to the door.

Andrew was late to pick her up, which meant they would be late to the gala and everyone would be looking at them when they walked in.

Her father wouldn't be impressed with that.

"It's about time..." The words died in her throat when she saw Andrew standing there, in a tuxedo. His blond hair was neat and combed back. He'd shaved and had put in his contacts. She wasn't used to seeing him without his black horn-rimmed glasses.

The tuxedo suited him. It was as if it was made for him, even though she knew that it was Keaka's tuxedo from the gala last year. Only it suited Andrew a lot more than it did her kid brother. And she knew she was gawking at him because she'd totally forgotten what she was going to scold him about.

"Wow," he said with a tone of awe. "You look amazing."

A blush crept up her cheeks. "Thanks. So do you."

He grinned and bowed slightly. "Thank you."

"So, you ready for this?" she asked, her voice trembling. "I'm nervous."

"I'm not nervous. I know how to work a crowd." He held out his arm. "Can I escort you to the limo?"

"You got a limo?" Now it was her turn to be surprised.

"I did," he said. "Seemed only fitting. Doesn't seem right for the Chief of Surgery's daughter to be arriving in my car. And the way you're dressed, it seems only fitting."

Lana took his arm and he escorted her down the drive to where a limo was waiting. The chauffeur opened the door and Andrew helped her down inside. She scooted over so he could climb in beside her.

Once the door was shut he pulled out of bottle of champagne and poured her a glass.

"I feel like I'm back in high school and going to prom."

He cocked an eyebrow. "You had a limo and a glass of champagne for your prom?"

"Well, my girlfriends did. I didn't go to prom, but I snuck the champagne in out of my dad's wine cellar. My only real act of defiance."

"Your only act of defiance?"

"I'm afraid so."

He winked and grinned, holding up his glass to hers. "Well, then, cheers."

"Cheers," she said and took a sip. "What about your prom?"

Andrew chuckled. "I didn't have a limo. A few buddies and I had a bonfire in the woods with our girlfriends after the dance. Our town was small, there really wasn't much to do except a bonfire in the woods. We scared the girls into thinking there were bears…got them to snuggle up closer."

She laughed as he winked. "And were there bears?"

"Probably. I grew up in northern Ontario, but black bears keep their distance for the most part."

"A bonfire sounds fun."

"We'll have to have one after we're married."

"You're making plans?" she asked, surprised again.

"You're the one that said a bonfire sounds fun and you have the perfect location for one."

"True." She took another sip of champagne. "Tomorrow will be a long day that I'm dreading."

"Me too," he said quietly and then he set down his champagne flute and pulled out a box. "This is for you."

Lana took the box from him. "What is it?"

"Your engagement ring," he said matter-of-factly.

Lana almost dropped it. She set down her champagne flute and stared at that black velvet box. Something that was just fake was becoming too real right now.

As if sensing that she was nervous, Andrew took the box out of her hand, opened it and pulled out a beautiful square-cut diamond. He slipped it on her left hand. His hands were so strong and steady, while hers trembled.

"You're shaking," he whispered. He ran his thumb in a circle over her knuckles.

"I wasn't expecting this." She wasn't expecting the rush of feeling tied to a piece of jewelry in a fake moment.

"Expecting what?" he asked gently, still holding her hand.

"The ring, of course."

"Well, we are engaged. And you demanded one, if I remember rightly."

"I suppose." She glanced up at him and looked into his eyes. Those blue eyes that seemed to melt right into her very soul. His touch was nice. Just the simple touch made her feel alive.

"It's a beautiful ring," she whispered.

Andrew leaned over and whispered in her ear, "Not as beautiful as the owner of the hand it graces."

She didn't know what to say to that. No one had ever paid a compliment to her like that before. It caught her off guard and she felt as if she was frozen to the spot. She was still in the moment, her pulse racing, trembling and yearning for his touch.

Lana realized she was holding her breath, waiting for a kiss, but it never came because the limo came to a stop in front of the resort where the gala was being held.

"I guess we're here," Andrew said, breaking their connection and letting go of her hand. "You ready for this?"

No.

"Yes. I think so."

The chauffeur opened the door and Andrew slid out. The chauffeur helped her get out of the limo and when she was standing next to Andrew he took her hand, which was heavy with a diamond on it.

It was all fake.

Not the ring, but the promise that it spoke to the rest of the world.

There was nothing sincere about this and it made her stomach twist with guilt. She didn't want to go inside and pretend, but she'd made a promise to Jack and Andrew. This was for the good of the hospital, for her younger brother.

It would make Jack happy.

It made her father happy.

It made everyone but her happy. Which was usual. So why was this so hard for her? What made it so different from anything else she did to appease her brother and father?

Lana didn't know. All she needed to remember tonight was to keep her wits about her so she didn't do something foolish which would ruin everything because, like it or not, tomorrow she was getting married.

For better or for worse.

CHAPTER SIX

ANDREW COULDN'T STOP watching Lana all night. She was so graceful and poised, it made him proud in a weird way, because really she wasn't anything to him. Perhaps a friend, but that was all.

Liar.

There was more—he wanted her. He wanted her like he hadn't wanted a woman in a long time. He'd always been attracted to her, but she'd never, ever showed interest in him. Then they'd had a moment in the limo when she'd trembled under his touch.

It sent a rush of heat through him.

Fired his blood.

Just watching her move through the different circles of people made him want her all the more.

I don't deserve her. Yet she would be his, under false pretenses.

Andrew took a sip of wine, his gaze focused on her as he watched her from the edge of the room. When Lana had opened the door and he'd seen her in that dress, it made the bikini look like a drab piece of cloth. There was more fabric to her dress, but it aroused him more than a two-piece bikini, because this dress accentuated all the right spots.

All of her curves. The color suited her. It brought out the richness in her dark eyes, but it was drab in comparison to her. Dr. Iolana Haole was the most gorgeous creature he'd ever laid eyes on and tomorrow she'd be his.

She's not yours. This marriage is fake, remember? And you don't deserve her.

Andrew shook that thought away, because it angered him.

"That is a beautiful ring you bought my daughter," Dr. Keaka Haole said as he came up beside him.

"Thank you, sir." Andrew turned to face the man he admired more than his own father. "Your daughter deserves the very best." And that wasn't a lie.

"I agree," Keaka said, grinning. "You'll make a fine husband and hopefully father one day."

Andrew choked on the wine he was taking a drink from, while Keaka chuckled softly.

"I'm sorry I caught you by surprise, Andrew, but I do hope to see grandchildren one day. To see my legacy continue."

"I can tell you, sir, that there is no plan in the immediate future for children." Andrew never wanted to be a father. That was not on his radar and never would be. His father was a terrible man and Andrew was never, ever going to bring a child into the world when he didn't know what a good father should be.

He wasn't going to screw up his kids' life the way his father had messed up his and his sister's life.

Didn't you *screw up your sister's life?*

"There may be no plan," Keaka said, interrupting his thoughts. "But surprises do happen. I didn't plan on either Iolana or Keaka Jr., but life has a way of throwing curveballs if you're not paying attention."

"So true." At least Andrew knew that the decision to have kids was something he could control. Even though he desperately wanted to take Lana into his bed, he wasn't going to, so that solved the kid issue. At least from his end.

"I'm looking forward to having you join our family, Andrew." Then Keaka looked uncomfortable. "I believe that you do care for her deeply. Unlike what happened a few years ago with David."

"Right," Andrew said, feeling awkward. He knew about Dr. David Preston and what had happened. He knew that Lana was painted as the pitiful creature and David a bit of a hero. David had used Lana as a way to further his career and wounded her pride—and broken her heart?

Aren't you doing the same?

The thought made guilt gnaw at him. Lana had believed that David loved her. There was no pretense of love between her and him, but still it wasn't real either.

"Thank you, sir." Andrew hoped Lana's father didn't notice the awkward tension.

"You can call me Keaka." Keaka grinned and took a drink from his wine glass. "You're an asset to the hospital, Andrew. I do wish you'd reconsider your surgical position. I know you performed surgery in Canada."

"Dr. Haole, you've seen my file; my shoulder was damaged and I had a botched surgery. There is no way I can competently hold a scalpel again."

Keaka narrowed his eyes, but the smile never

left his lips. "You know who could fix that botched shoulder?"

"You. I know. You're the best," Andrew said.

"I am good, but Lana could fix it. It's too bad you two fell in love and are getting married so now she'll never be able to operate on you."

"Yes, that's a shame." He was lying through his teeth, but it was a good excuse to get people to back off about his shoulder and his surgical privileges. He was a good physician. He didn't need operating room privileges.

Yes, you do. You miss it.

"Well, I would like you to teach our residents the famous Tremblay flap procedure. At least in the simulation lab," Keaka said.

"I'll think about it, sir." Andrew set down his glass of wine as the music started playing a nice jazzy slow song. "If you'll excuse me, Keaka, I think I'm going to grab your daughter and take her for a dance."

Keaka grinned and held up his wine glass as Andrew made his way through the crowd. He was glad to put some distance between him and his boss. Or rather his future father-in-law. Who was asking way too many questions he was not comfortable with.

It was bad enough Keaka Sr. knew about his shoulder. At least no one beyond human resources and Keaka Sr. knew. Patient confidentiality was a blessing. He didn't want Lana to pity him the way he pitied himself.

Lana turned the moment he came up to the group.

Her dark eyes twinkling, she was still smiling. "Andrew?"

"Would you care to dance?" He held out his hand, his pulse thundering in his ears. He wanted to kiss her and he didn't know why that compulsion came over him.

"I don't dance," she said quickly.

"Tonight you do." And, without taking no for an answer, he took her hand and pulled her out onto the dance floor, spinning her around and then pulling her close as they danced together. "Whoa, I didn't realize how tall you are in those heels."

"Well, I think we're the same height, so yes, the heels do give me a bit of an advantage. I usually wear flats."

"We're not the same height, or else you'd be really towering over me."

"Would it make you feel better if I took my shoes off?" she teased.

"Perhaps, but I don't think that's proper decorum."

She cocked a finely arched brow. "Oh? And what's proper decorum, plastic milk crate man?"

Andrew laughed at her dig. "I'm totally bringing those to your house. Correction, our house."

"You are not!" Then she laughed. "I'm totally wigging out about tomorrow."

"It'll be fine." He ran his hand over her bare back, revelling in the silky-soft feel of her skin. Goose pimples rose under his light touch.

Where else would he bring out this reaction in her?

He was glad he was having such an effect on her.

"Don't," she whispered, her voice hitching slightly.

"Why?" He stopped anyways, though he didn't want to.

"Because…just…"

"I'm sorry, I can't help it. You're a beautiful woman." He wanted to lean in and kiss her, but he was holding back. This wasn't real. He couldn't have her. He had to respect the boundaries.

"Excuse me, Dr. Haole?"

Andrew inwardly thanked the hotel event captain for interrupting this moment. Andrew let go of Lana.

"Yes?" she asked.

"There's a phone call for you from the hospital. They said it was urgent."

"Okay."

"I'll wait right here," Andrew said.

She nodded, but wouldn't look him in the eye. He hoped he hadn't made her angry. He hoped that she wouldn't change her mind about helping him. He hoped that he hadn't ruined it all.

"This is Dr. Haole speaking." Lana tried to focus on the call that was coming through and tried to ignore the sensation that still was burned into her skin from Andrew's light touch. It had felt good. She wanted more. She wanted him to kiss her. Her heart was still racing and she had to get control of herself or she might do something impulsive.

She listened to the resident explain that the patient's collarbone was badly fractured, and the broken bone had punctured a lung. The lung was repaired, but the collarbone needed to be addressed. The collarbone would have to be repaired with screws and plates, because the fracture was so bad.

"Tell Dr. Young I'll be right there to fix the collarbone."

"The other lung is damaged and we may have to cut the other side of the clavicle to remove a sharp object embedded into the patient's shoulder."

Lana growled into the receiver, "You do not cut that man's clavicle without me there. Do you understand, Doctor? Cutting the clavicle is not the answer."

"Yes, Dr. Haole."

"I'll be there in ten minutes. Keep him stable." Lana ended the call.

"Is everything okay?" Andrew asked, coming up behind her.

"No," she said. "I have to get back to the hospital or Dr. Young is going to break the other side of a patient's clavicle because Dr. Young may be a fantastic general surgeon, but she's not an orthopedic one."

Andrew winced and then nodded. "Okay, let's get you to the hospital. You tell your dad why we're leaving and I'll get us a ride there."

“Sounds good.” Lana made her way through the crowd. Her father had had a few too many drinks with a few other orthopedic surgeons who were attending the gala; she was probably the only one, besides her resident, in the vicinity who’d had barely anything to drink. Even David, across the room, was teetering and his new conquest looked none too pleased. Although he wasn’t an orthopedic surgeon. He was a neurologist.

Good.

At least she was responsible.

As always.

The last thing she drank was that sip of champagne before Andrew had slipped this ring on her finger over three hours ago. A cup of coffee before she scrubbed in would chase away any remnants, but really there was nothing in her system. She was the only one who could do this surgery.

Her father wished her well and she was headed straight for the entrance they’d come in. Andrew was pacing by the door.

“A cab is waiting.”

“Good, let’s get out of here.”

Andrew helped her into the cab and gave instructions to the driver while Lana pulled off her expensive necklace and earrings and put them in her evening bag. In her bag she carried a hair elastic, so while the cab negotiated the streets from the resort to the hospital she quickly braided her hair and put it up. All she had to do now was slip out of her dress and shoes in her office, throw on some scrubs and scrub in.

Then she remembered the ring on her left hand, glinting in the street lamps that they raced past. She didn't want to take it off and lose it.

"Pin it to your scrubs," Andrew said.

"What?" she asked.

"I saw you staring at the ring. The way you were frowning at it, you seemed confused about what to do with it, like you forgot it was there when you took off your other jewelry."

"I did forget," she said sheepishly.

"It's okay, Lana." He nodded. "Pin it to your scrubs; that's what I see the nurses do all the time. They pin it over their heart."

She tried not to roll her eyes. "I'll do just that."

He grinned. "That's my girl."

"Don't call me that!"

"Snookums?"

"Didn't we already have this conversation, Tremblay?"

He chuckled. "I suppose we did."

The cab pulled up in front of the hospital. Andrew took care of the fare while Lana got out and raced toward her office. Andrew ran after her. As she tried to undo her dress she realized she couldn't reach the zipper but, before she could curse in annoyance, she felt Andrew's hand on her back.

"Let me help," he whispered.

Her body shivered in delight as he undid the hook that was just a bit above her waist and then pulled the zipper down. It was such an intimate thing to do and it heated her blood just with the thought of him touching her.

Of Andrew doing something so intimate. Something only a lover or husband might do.

Well, he's almost your husband.

"Thank you," she managed to squeak out.

"No problem." He undid his bow tie, slipping it off, and then took off his jacket. Her pulse began to race and a bunch of naughty thoughts crept across her mind.

It had been so long since she'd had any sort of physical contact with a man. She'd never really missed it before. Didn't care for it much when she had been intimate with a man, but being close to

Andrew, getting to know him and being so attracted to him was giving her pause.

Maybe it wouldn't be so bad with him? Just once.

Don't think like that. You can't think like that. He's off-limits.

She had been expecting him to leave, but he was still standing there. "Are you going to get into a set of scrubs too?"

"Yeah… I think I would like to watch, if you don't mind, and not from the galley." He was pale when he managed to get the words out. "Do you have an extra set of scrubs in here?"

"Only women's, but I'm sure there's some larger ones in the residents' lounge."

He nodded. "I'll see you down on the OR floor."

Once he left, Lana was able to take a deep breath and calm her erratic pulse. She had to get everything under control because she had to focus on the surgery at hand. A clavicle that was broken and protruding, lung damage and the other clavicle that might need to be broken surgically to remove something that was imbedded into the patient's other shoulder? This was going to be a long, tricky surgery.

Lana hoped that the other side of the clavicle

didn't need to be broken. That the object could be removed and then she could just repair the side of the clavicle that was broken. Right now she had to get her game face on.

This was what she lived for.

This was what she'd dedicated her whole life to. It was her passion. But a hospital setting had never been her passion. Lana had wanted to travel the world, work in third world countries doing orthopedic repairs.

Actually, she'd wanted to live out of the back of a rucksack, much like Andrew had been doing. Only that wasn't what her father had wanted for her. If he was going to spend money to send her to prestigious schools like Princeton, then she was going to become a world class surgeon. He was going to groom her to take over the hospital one day.

It just wasn't what she wanted, but it was what she was fated for.

Lana had given up hoping for anything different. This was her life now and, as much as she felt trapped by the way her father had planned out her life, at least she could still practice surgery. At least she was still helping people.

She took a calming breath. First she pinned her

engagement ring to her scrubs like Andrew had suggested. It was heavy over her heart and she was very aware of it.

Focus.

As she stepped into the scrub room she watched the trauma surgeons work on the patient. The man had been impaled by a metal pole. And she winced when she saw it.

"It's nasty," Andrew said, coming up beside her, scrubbing in. He had to be sterile too, even if he was only observing.

"It doesn't look pleasant." She shook off her hands then grabbed a paper towel to dry them.

"I'm glad you took my advice about the ring."

"Now everyone will see it," she muttered.

"The surgical gown will cover it." Then he leaned over, grinning in that charming sexy way that always made her weak in the knees. "Besides, everyone knows we're engaged. Unless, of course, you're afraid that a token, such as a ring, makes you appear weak."

Lana rolled her eyes. "You ready to come in there?" she asked.

He frowned. "Why wouldn't I be?"

"This is the first time I've seen you in the operating room since you came here. You've always avoided it since I've known you. Though I've noticed you in the gallery, I was surprised when you suggested you'd come in and observe."

The frown intensified. His eyes narrowed and she knew she'd pushed him again. She'd pushed those invisible buttons that he was so sensitive about.

"Do you not want me in there?" He spun it around, trying to change the focus.

"I want you in there. I would love if you assisted me."

"No surgical privileges, except observation, remember?"

"I haven't forgotten." She headed into the operating room, shuddering at the change in temperature. The OR was chilly and she'd been in a packed gala for most of the night. Not to mention that it had been muggy outside as well. Even though she knew the operating room was kept at a lower temperature, her body still was shocked and she couldn't help but shiver as a scrub nurse helped her on with her surgical gown and gloves.

"Sorry to tear you away from your gala, Dr. Haole, but I figured that you might be the only orthopedic surgeon in a five mile radius who would be sober enough to help me." Dr. Young was giving her a dig.

Lana bit her tongue. Figuratively. "I am the orthopedic surgeon on call, so your assumption would be correct, Dr. Young."

Dr. Young snorted in response but continued working on the punctured lung. "I'll soon be done here and then you can go about repairing the clavicle."

"What about the object in his other shoulder? Will you remove that?"

"I would like to, but I think that I will have to break the other clavicle to remove it and you gave strict instructions for us not to touch it." The tone was sanctimonious. Dr. Young was older than her and had been a trauma surgeon overseas while she'd been serving the country. She'd probably done this on her own, but when it came to orthopedic procedures at this hospital Lana oversaw them all.

No one was touching the unbroken part of the clavicle until she'd gotten a good look at it.

"Do we have any recent imaging?" Lana asked.

"Here, Dr. Haole," a resident said, lighting up the screen to show X-rays.

Andrew walked into the operating room.

"It looks like the object has lodged next to the acromioclavicular joint and the clavicle."

Lana nodded. "It's lucky it wasn't dislocated, but it's jammed in there."

"The main concern Dr. Young had was whether dislodging it would damage the lung," the resident, Dr. Page, said.

"If I manage the dislocation I don't need to break the clavicle. If I dislocate it from the joint in a controlled manner we can remove the object without damaging the lung and repair the joint with this side of the clavicle intact."

"I agree," Andrew said. "I've done this before."

"Are you certain?" Dr. Young called from the table, where she was finishing up her part of the job. "I don't want to have to come back and clean up your mess when you damage the lung."

"Then you don't have to. I've repaired a lung before or Dr. Page can help me. I'm sure he's capable of it as well."

Dr. Young shook her head. Lana knew she was overstepping some boundaries, but she didn't know why Dr. Young had her knickers in a knot over her. Of course, when didn't Dr. Young have her knickers in a knot?

"Since you're so confident in Dr. Page's ability, I am finished here." Dr. Young handed over her surgical tools and walked away.

Lana gritted her teeth but didn't say anything. Dr. Young was so passive-aggressive and didn't trust anyone unless they'd been doing surgery for at least fifteen years. And it wasn't as if her father had instilled a lot of confidence. He'd overseen most of her surgeries like this in the past and Dr. Young was digging at her for being the daughter of the chief.

"What a diva," Andrew whispered under his breath.

Lana snorted as she took the lead surgeon's spot. "Dr. Page, would you assist me?"

"Yes, Dr. Haole!"

"Get a surgical gown on and gloves."

Dr. Page nodded and headed over to a scrub nurse to get gowned up. He was eager and Lana couldn't begrudge the resident that, though Lana would rather have Andrew, who had done this before. She'd rather he'd assist her, but Andrew made no move to assist. He stood where the X-rays were, watching her as she went to work.

It was a delicate procedure, but it would be the only way to dislodge the object from the patient's shoulder without damaging the joint, breaking the clavicle again or damaging the lungs. Lana took a deep breath and glanced over at Andrew again. She had a moment of uncertainty. She hadn't done this procedure a lot of times. Especially without her father here. Whenever she came into the operating room with something like this, her father insisted on assisting.

If she screwed this up…

Don't think about it.

Andrew nodded. "You got this."

Just like that, his belief in her entered her and it shocked her how much he calmed her in that moment. No one had ever been able to calm her down so fast. It was scary, but she also liked it. And she was surprised by how much she liked it.

Lana took a deep breath and waited for Dr. Page to join her at the table. The X-rays were wheeled over so that she could get a closer look at the object. Then the fluoroscope was turned on, so she could see the joints in the shoulder. After the object which had impaled the patient was removed, then she would repair the dislocation and then fix the broken side of the clavicle. The patient would be in the long haul for physiotherapy and would be in a lot of pain.

Tonight would be a long night. She just hoped

that she got a bit of sleep so she didn't have dark circles under her eyes for tomorrow night's wedding.

"Are you ready, Dr. Haole?" Dr. Page asked.

"Yes. Let's get this patient on the road to recovery." She took a deep breath and held out her hand to the scrub nurse. "Scalpel."

CHAPTER SEVEN

RUN.

That was his first thought, but he couldn't do that to Lana. Instead he pulled at his collar, which felt too tight. Stifling, almost.

Andrew had worn this tuxedo last night at the gala. It hadn't bothered him then, but now, standing on the beach with the ocean behind him and a bunch of strangers sitting on either side of the torch-strewn aisle with a minister and Jack, it suddenly felt that the collar on the tuxedo was shrinking.

Run. Just run.

Jack leaned over. "Stop pulling at it, Andrew."

"It's bothering me," Andrew whispered, but he continued to fiddle with it.

"Yeah, 'cos you're pulling at it." Jack shook his head. "Why are you so nervous?"

Andrew didn't answer Jack's question and stopped fidgeting. He was still tired from watching Lana perform that surgery last night—a surgery he was all too familiar with—and his arm twinged, reminding him of his accident.

"Meghan, you should buckle up."

"I'm fine. I just have to take off my coat... Oh, my God. Andrew! The moose!"

Andrew winced as the sound of screaming filled his head.

If only his surgeon had done to him what Lana had pulled off so beautifully. Instead they had cut the metal out, tearing his joints and muscles around his shoulders. His shoulder blade had been shattered and pieced together incorrectly. He was lucky to have his arm still.

Yeah, lucky.

"You should've been the one to die!"

"There was a moose, Dad. I couldn't..."

"I don't care. You should've died. Not her. You killed her."

He'd watched Lana throughout that surgery with absolute awe and admiration. In the moment before the surgery started she'd looked at him for reassurance. In that moment she'd trusted him. It had been so long since he'd felt that kind of connection with someone.

It was unnerving.

As soon as the surgery was over he'd left, because he'd had to put some distance between them. She stirred something in him. Something that scared him. The problem was he was marrying her. There was no place to hide.

There were so many emotions running through him right now.

When he'd first thought of marrying to stay in the country he'd had no real emotional attachment or feeling about Lana other than attraction. She'd always been icy to him. She annoyed him and he knew that he annoyed her.

They were civil, polite, but they hadn't had much interaction. So he'd never really worried about the ramifications of any emotional attachment to her. He'd figured that he'd be able to walk away after the year and go on with his life.

Until recently. Now, he was enjoying her company. He wasn't so indifferent to her. He was setting himself up for something dangerous.

This is not real. It's platonic.

Though right now, standing here, this wedding felt real. It was legal and real in that sense, but there was something more.

Sophie Haole, Lana's stepmother, had made this wedding as real as any he'd seen. Torches were arranged in the sand, forming an aisle, and amongst the guests there was no one he recognized. Andrew wasn't surprised by that really, since the only friends he had were Jack and a couple of other guys he trained.

He had no family here. His family didn't care much about him.

The sun was setting, slipping into the ocean, and the wind picked up, causing the flames on the torches to flicker.

Deep breath.

Then he thought again about turning and running, except it would humiliate Lana. She was in this as deep as he was. He had to stick it out. There was no going back now.

The music started. Even though everything about him was telling him to run, he stood his ground. Then he saw Lana and everything that told him to flee was silenced in one quick moment.

In fact, he forgot to breathe.

Oh, my God.

She was beautiful.

Breathtaking.

And he knew then and there that he was in big trouble.

Dr. Haole was beaming as he walked Lana

down the aisle toward him. Lana, under the veil, seemed a bit shell-shocked. It looked as if he wasn't the only one who was unsure and terrified. A smile crept across his face and then he just couldn't stop smiling as she came closer.

Suddenly he was ridiculously happy and he didn't know why and couldn't remember the last time he'd been this happy.

"You're an idiot!" Meghan had screeched happily as they'd walked out of the movie theater.

"Oh, come on, you're happy to have me home, admit it!" He'd slung his arm around his sister.

"I am. I've missed you. It's been terrible here."

"Well, that will all change. You'll come back to Vancouver now that you're going to school there. You can live with me. I'll take care of you, Meghan."

"Promise?"

"I promise."

Only he'd broken that promise that night.

He wouldn't break his promise to Jack.

When Dr. Haole placed Lana's hand in his, hers was trembling.

"You okay?" Andrew whispered as her father stepped away.

"Perhaps." Then she smiled. "What happened to our simple wedding at City Hall?"

"Nothing about us is simple, it seems," he teased.

They both laughed at that, melting away all the tension and uncertainty about what they were about to do. The officiant stepped up and began the ceremony. Andrew was only half listening. All he could think about was how beautiful Lana was.

She glowed.

He wasn't sure if it was the waning sunlight or the dress, but all Andrew could think about was that she was going to be his wife.

Mine.

Only she wasn't his. There would be no honeymoon. No night of passion between them. Even if he wanted it. Lana would only be his on paper. He would never be able to take her in his arms and make love to her. This deal wasn't forever. There was an end date.

An expiry.

"Do you, Andrew Francis Tremblay, take Iolana Sarah Haole as your lawfully wedded wife?"

"I do." It shocked him how easily the words

came out. He had been worried he wouldn't be able to say it so smoothly when it was all a lie.

"Do you, Iolana Sarah Haole, take Andrew Francis Tremblay as your lawfully wedded husband?"

"I do," she whispered. She squeezed his hand after she said the words, as if she too had been worried about the vows. It was nice not to feel alone.

"Do you have the rings?" the officiant asked.

Jack handed him her wedding ring, while her stepmother handed her a gold band that would be his. He slipped the band on her finger and she slipped the thick gold band on his hand. It was heavy. It felt awkward. Like a shackle.

"Then, by the power invested in me by the State of Hawaii, I now pronounce you man and wife. You may kiss your bride."

His pulse roared in his ears as he lifted the veil. *Just one kiss to seal it. That's all.*

Her dark eyes were twinkling in the twilight. They were wide as she looked at him. He'd wanted to do this. He wanted this, badly. So he cupped her face and bent his head down to kiss her. Electric heat, like a burn, moved through him. And he knew as the kiss ended and everyone clapped that one kiss would never be enough.

Lana was still in a daze as Andrew took her hand and they moved down the aisle. People were tossing flower petals at them. The memory of Andrew's kiss was still burned into the flesh of her lips. The thing was, she wanted more.

Every time she got closer to Andrew, the more she wanted. She glanced down at her hand to see the wedding band and it shocked her. She'd only got her engagement ring last night at the gala and now she had a wedding band on her hand. It felt foreign, but she liked the look of it as well—and she'd thought she would never wear a wedding band, because she had no interest in the idea of matrimony.

Or at least didn't think that it would happen.

"You're still shaking," he said as they headed down the path to the tent on the golf course overlooking the ocean where their reception was waiting.

"I think I'm in a bit of shock. Did that really just happen?" she asked.

"I'm afraid so." He kissed her hand as they walked the path. "Thank you, by the way."

"For what?"

"For marrying me." And he was serious. This wasn't a tease or a light-hearted moment. This was a moment of sincerity, which made her stomach flip flop with anticipation. She didn't know what to say, but could feel blood rushing to her cheeks and she looked away.

"No problem."

"You're stuck with me now," he teased, which eased the tension.

"I could say the same. Thank you for the ring, by the way. Both the rings."

"You deserve it." They waited outside as the rest of the guests filtered in from a different direction. "Your stepmother went all-out."

"I told you that she would. It's her profession and I guess I'm her showpiece."

"A luau, though? I thought your father didn't like the gimmicky touristy things people expect about Hawaii."

"Usually, but he likes luaus. What my father wants he gets," Lana sighed. She'd really had no say in it all. Ever since Andrew had announced their engagement in the staff meeting, it had felt as if she didn't have much say in a whole lot of things. Her father had taken over—as usual. Her whole life, she had been dictated to.

All she'd wanted was a simple wedding. She hadn't even picked out her dress.

You didn't even want this, though.

Which was true, so she shouldn't be saddened by her father planning it. It wasn't real after all.

"What did you want?" Andrew asked and it surprised her he asked. No one ever asked her what she wanted. She didn't know what to say.

"City Hall."

He chuckled. "No, I mean what did you really want? What did you dream about as a young girl?"

That was something she hadn't thought about or even entertained since she was about ten years old. She'd forgotten about those dreams. That was when her mother was around still and she could just be a kid.

Since her mother left she'd really let go of all her childhood memories. All those hopes and dreams and the make-believe. When her mother left was when she grew more pragmatic. That was when she'd started playing peacekeeper and parent. It was when she'd had to grow up.

"Actually, I wanted to be married on the beach, but there were a lot more unicorns involved."

Andrew laughed. "No luau?"

She wrinkled her nose. "No, pizza dinner would've been nice. And root beer floats."

"That sounds like fun," he said.

"A lot of fun. Then honeymoon in a castle, but I suppose this resort is good enough."

"It would be nice to have a couple of nights here," he agreed.

Then her cheeks heated as she thought of a couple nights here alone. "You know we're spending our wedding night here."

A strange look passed across his face. One of restraint and fear.

Before he could respond, Sophie opened the flap to their private tent. "We're ready to announce you two now."

"Okay." Andrew cleared his throat and took Lana's hand. "You ready for this?"

"As ready as I'll ever be." She squeezed his hand as they were led into the reception area, where they were announced as Dr. and Mrs. Tremblay, which made her grit her teeth just a bit. She was a doctor too, but her dad was old-fashioned. Then the Polynesian dancers that her father hired gave them a traditional welcome.

After the dance they were led to the head table, where her father welcomed everyone. Lana just sat there like a centerpiece. She hated the attention. The reception was a blur because it felt a bit unreal and she felt guilty for tricking her loved ones.

Everyone was enjoying the food, including Andrew, but it tasted like sawdust in her mouth. She just wanted this whole farce to be over and done with. This wasn't real and she was tired of acting. After dinner and some more entertainment, a band started playing and Andrew turned to her.

"It's time for our dance," Andrew stated.

"Our what?"

"As man and wife—our first dance." Andrew stood and held out his hand. "What do you say, Mrs. Tremblay?"

"Seriously? It's Dr. Tremblay," she teased. At least the wedding reception would soon be over. Then they could get back to normal.

You mean being lonely normal?

Andrew chuckled and she took his hand as she stood. He led her out onto the dance floor and pulled her close as they moved across it.

"I do enjoy dancing with you, Lana."

"We've been dancing a lot lately. I don't think I've danced this much in my life," she admitted.

"Are you complaining?" he asked.

"No, I'm not." She gazed into his blue eyes because she did like dancing, especially with him. "For someone who spent a lot of time at bonfires drinking beer and seducing women you're a very good dancer."

"Well, the girls did like to dance around the fire as well. And I didn't mind holding them close, but I like holding you close better."

She blushed and then wondered how much was true. They were out in public and had to put on a show. Andrew was a known flirt.

It's all pretend.

For once, though, she didn't care. She craved the human touch and she just wanted to have a stolen moment with a man she found attractive. Just one moment where she wasn't responsible, sensible, boring Iolana.

"You okay?" he asked.

"Why?"

"You seem sad all of a sudden."

"No. I'm not sad, I'm just tired. The surgery

from yesterday was so long and late into the night. I'm still not rested enough."

"Want to slip out of here early?"

"People will know we're missing. It's our wedding." Though she desperately wanted to. She was done pretending for all these friends of her father.

"Exactly, it's our wedding. People are partying. Let's go and we'll get you some peace and quiet."

Lana saw her family and friends were enjoying the party. They could escape. She already had the key card to the room. She just needed to get away from all of this.

"Let's go," Lana said. She wanted out of here. This was all too overwhelming.

Andrew nodded and they snuck out of the reception. She'd never snuck out of one of her father's parties before.

It was kind of thrilling to rebel this way.

She never rebelled.

They took a back stairwell in the resort to the honeymoon suite, which was ready and waiting for them. The terrace doors had been opened and faced the ocean, where a full moon was reflected on the water. The palms were swaying and their gentle sound was mixed with the faint strains of the band from the reception.

There was champagne and chocolate-covered strawberries. The large king-sized bed was strewn with rose petals. It oozed romance.

Her pulse began to race. This room was supposed to be for two people in love.

Not for two fakers.

"Wow, your stepmother likes to go all-out." Andrew whistled. "This is something."

"Yeah, that's Sophie."

Andrew undid his bow tie and unbuttoned his shirt. Her heart hammered as she thought about him getting undressed. It had been so long since she'd been intimate with a man. Completely out of character, she was longing for his touch. Being in his arms on the dance floor had been nice. So nice. Comforting.

"You're getting undressed?" she teased.

"The collar was too tight." He then slipped off the jacket and rolled up the sleeves of the shirt, but still kept the vest on. She was disappointed, but it was probably for the best. He wandered out on the terrace and Lana poured champagne, kicked off her shoes and followed him outside. She handed him a flute.

"Thanks," he said and then took a sip, leaning against the balcony.

"Sorry it's not beer." Then she nodded toward their reception on the green. "There's a bonfire where they were cooking the pig down on the beach."

"Nice." Andrew held up his champagne flute to clink with hers. "Sorry there're no unicorns."

And he winked at her, his blue eyes sparkling in the dim light.

"It's quite all right." She drank down her champagne and then leaned over the terrace. "At least we have a nice view." The ocean was like glass with a full moon rising over the water, the palm trees swaying and the flicker of flames against the night sky made her sigh.

"That's not the view I'm enjoying."

She glanced over at him and he was staring at her. It sent a delicious shiver down her spine. She wanted him. Rarely did she take what she wanted. She was too shy about men she was attracted to. And David had completely shattered her self-esteem and heart. Andrew was a playboy like David.

Yet they were married. They were adults. Why couldn't she just indulge this one time?

She set down her flute and walked over to him. He watched her as she stood in front of him.

Lana kissed him then, swept away in the fairy tale fantasy of it all. The kiss was gentle at first, but then it deepened into something more dangerous. His mouth opening and his tongue entwining with hers. One hand went into her hair and the other around her waist as he pulled her tight against him. She knew then he was feeling what she was feeling. He wanted her just as much as she wanted him.

Why couldn't they indulge this once? Why did she always have to play by the rules?

People had casual sex all the time. They were consenting adults and she wanted this. She didn't have to give him her heart. Just her body and just for this night.

Heck, she'd wanted this the first day she'd met him. Even when he annoyed her. Even though she knew he was bad for her.

The kiss ended but Andrew didn't let her go.

"Andrew, I want this."

"Are you sure?"

"Yes."

"I don't want…" He trailed off. "I want you too, Lana but…"

"It doesn't have to mean anything, Andrew. I know this isn't forever and I'm fine with that. I'm not expecting more. If I was, I wouldn't have done this."

"Okay." He sounded a bit off.

"I won't get hurt, Andrew. Why can't we just have this one moment together?"

"Lana, I…"

She kissed him again. "I want you, Andrew. I'm sure about this. Make love to me."

"I can't. I want… I can't." Andrew pushed past her and left the terrace.

Lana stood there, stunned, until she heard the door slam. Then she just felt stupid and tears stung her eyes. She didn't know what she'd been thinking.

All she'd been thinking about was her need.

How lonely she was.

She shouldn't have taken the chance.

Every time she took a chance she was burned.

CHAPTER EIGHT

LANA'S REQUEST HAD caught him off guard, but he wasn't displeased by it. Not at all. It was just that he couldn't. He'd just never expected it from her. She was always was so careful, guarded, but the more time he was spending with her, the more he realized a hot fiery passion burned beneath the surface.

And that was something he wanted to explore, but he had a sneaking suspicion that if he tasted this once, he was going to want more and more. So, even though it killed him, he left the room. Walked the beach, far away from the wedding, to calm his senses, but it didn't work because all he could think about was Lana's lips pressed against his.

The feeling of her in his arms.

And her begging him to make love to her.

You can't.

Although he wanted to.

After what seemed like an eternity he returned

to the room. Hoping that everything had blown over, that she might be already asleep even, but instead he saw her sitting on the couch, a flute of champagne in her hand. She turned to look at him when he shut the door and he could see the tearstains on her cheeks.

Pain hit him hard.

He'd hurt her.

"Oh, I didn't expect you to come back," she said quietly and she wiped the tears from her face.

"I just needed a moment to myself."

"I see," she said quietly. Then she sighed. "Well, I think I'm going to turn in."

"Lana, I think we need to talk," he said.

"What is there to talk about?" She frowned. "You didn't want me and you have nothing to apologize about. I'm the one that wanted to step out of the boundaries we set. Not you."

"No, that's not it."

"What do you mean?" she asked, confused.

"I want you too, Lana. It's not for lack of desiring you. I want you. More than anything." And, though he knew that he shouldn't, he closed the distance between them and kissed her, fully expecting her to pull back from him the way that he had pulled from her, but she didn't. Instead she melted into his arms and he knew that he was a lost man.

There would be no walking away from her again tonight.

He was so weak.

Without asking any more questions, he scooped her up in his arms and carried her back into the room. He laid her down on the bed and kissed her again, pressing his weight against her, but he hated the fact there were so many layers of clothes that were separating them.

He wanted nothing between them.

All he wanted was just skin on skin. No words, just raw need driving their passion. Lana seemed to be feeling the same thing as he was because her fingers began to undo the buttons of his vest and then his shirt, but he didn't want to be the only one completely naked—he wanted to undress her.

And he didn't want to get her dress ruined.

"Let's get that dress off you and then we can work on my tuxedo."

She grinned at him and stood up. He spun her around, but let his hands linger on her bare back, just reveling in the silky softness of it. Lana sighed and where he touched there was a trail of goose pimples. He loved the way her body responded to his.

It made him want her even more.

He undid the clasp and unzipped the dress. It was similar to the dress she'd worn last night, only this one was ivory and of a heavier material.

Lana shrugged her shoulders out and the dress fell to the floor, pooling at her feet. Andrew was not prepared for the visual onslaught of her standing there in bridal lingerie. The slip, the garter belt and stockings, the bustier.

She turned around to face him, those dark eyes sparkling with that fire he knew was buried underneath. He could see the blush that he so adored creep up from her slender neck and blossom in her cheeks.

"Now it's your turn." And she undid the rest of the buttons on his shirt. She pulled it down off his arms and then ran her fingers over his chest. The mere light touch of her fingers on him sent a jolt of heat from where she touched straight to his groin.

He was so aroused by her.

And he couldn't remember ever having wanted a woman so much that a groan slipped past his lips. Her hands slid in the waistband of his trousers and she undid the button and then the fly. He shimmied out of his pants and then pushed her back on the bed before removing his socks. All that was left between them now was their undergarments, but those would soon be gone.

He kissed her again. Hungrily.

"I hate to break this up, but do you have protection?" she asked.

Crap.

Usually he carried one in his wallet and he couldn't remember if he'd put it in his pocket or not. Even though sex was the last thing he had been expecting with Lana, because he didn't want to push something he knew could be so dangerous for both of them.

As luck would have it, he did have his wallet and there was one.

He pulled it out. "Yep."

"Thank goodness."

"No one is more thankful than me." He joined her back on the bed. "Now, where were we?"

She cupped his face. "I think we were here."

The kiss fired his blood, but he sensed that there was no nervousness that was there before. The uncertainty that seemed to sometimes plague

Lana when dealing with things that were beyond the scope of medicine and only dealt with emotion.

There was no uncertainty now. She seemed to know exactly what she wanted and that made him burn for her.

This was the confident Lana that he knew in the hospital.

The one who knew exactly what she wanted. Although he liked the one that was vulnerable, he liked this version of her as well. As they were kissing she ran his hands over his back and her hands paused on the scar, touching it gently as if she was trying to figure out what it was, but she didn't linger long.

She didn't stop and question him. Which was a relief. He didn't want to talk about that right now. All he wanted to do was focus on this moment. He wanted to feel with her. He wanted to forget everything.

He wanted to bury himself inside her.

Not soon enough all that remained between them was gone. And it was just the two of them, heart to heart. She was completely bared to him.

When he ran his hands over her body, she responded, arching her back. He wanted to take her now, but he wanted her to give him a sign, he wanted her to be ready. He wanted her to want him as much as burned for her.

Lana didn't need to say a word to let him know that she was ready, with a slight arch of her hips and her legs wrapped around him. He didn't kiss her in that moment, instead he gazed deep into her eyes, his fingers entwined with hers as he entered her.

It was almost too much for him to hold back. And he couldn't recall any time before this moment. It had never been like this with anyone else.

It scared him, but thrilled him. He hadn't had such a rush, such a thrill since he was surfing. That had been when he was truly free.

Lana made him feel truly free.

She came around him and it wasn't long until he was joining her. He rolled over on his back, trying to catch his breath, and she snuggled in beside him. Her hand on his chest. The way that Lana had made him feel things terrified him.

Things that he never wanted to feel with anyone.

He liked living his life alone. And he wondered why he'd even agreed to this marriage. Right now, holding her in his arms in their bridal suite, he was scared about how he was feeling. How in one moment Lana had got to him when no one else had been able to.

Except his sister, but when she'd died and his family shut him out, he'd felt that he didn't deserve this. He felt guilty.

"Are you okay?" Lana asked, propping herself up on one elbow, her black hair cascading over her shoulders, making it impossible to shut her out.

"I'm fine." He grinned at her.

"That was great. Thank you."

He grinned. "I've never been thanked before."

"Well, I was taught to have manners," she teased.

Andrew laughed and then kissed her. "You're welcome then."

"So, the scar?"

Andrew stiffened under her. "What about it?"

"Now you're definitely not okay," she said.

"I don't like to talk about it."

"What happened?"

"An accident."

"Is that why you won't operate?"

Andrew sighed and pushed her away. He got up out of bed and pulled on his pants. He didn't look back at Lana because he didn't want to be tempted to be drawn back into bed.

She was so tempting, but she was delving into a conversation that he wasn't comfortable having. His accident happened, it ended his surfing career and it ended his surgical career. It was done. There was no need to discuss.

He was all too aware of the consequences of accidents. And the last time he'd tried to talk about it, about his sister's death, he'd been shot down by his parents. Not that they'd always had the best relationship, but they blamed him for her death.

They said he'd killed her.

His best friend. The only person who had been there for him, his beloved baby sister. He'd lost his family back then and learned a valuable lesson—hide your emotions. Don't talk about painful things.

It was better this way.

Yet Lana was prying into something that he wasn't willing to talk about.

"Andrew, I didn't mean to upset you."

"You didn't upset me." He was lying through his teeth.

"I just know that it pains you and it's a significant scar. I just want to help."

"There's nothing you can do."

"But…"

"I don't want to talk about it, Lana," he snapped. "It's done. There's no use in talking about something you can't change."

She frowned and then hugged her knees. "You're right. Talking never really solves anything, does it?"

It was sarcasm.

And, just like that, the magic of their moment was shattered.

There was a wall between them again, but the wall needed to be there. It would keep them both safe.

You mean it will keep you safe.

He shook that thought from his mind as he slipped on his shoes and buttoned up his shirt.

"Where are you going?" she asked.

"For another walk."

Lana nodded, but she wasn't looking at him. "Okay. I think I'll have a rest. I'm still tired from that surgery yesterday."

"Sounds good." Andrew sighed inwardly and left the room. "I'll see you later."

He hated himself right now. He hated hurting her, but she was treading on dangerous ground.

You mean you are.

* * *

Lana knew that she had been treading on dangerous ground. Any time she'd mentioned his shoulder pain in the past he'd thrown up a wall. Why had she thought that this time would be different? She was beating herself up that she'd asked him about his scar.

He'd mentioned an accident, but she couldn't help but wonder what had happened. The first thing that came to mind as she thought about the way the scar was that his shoulder had been shattered and the repair hadn't gone well.

Or at least he didn't think so.

And maybe it hadn't, given the pain he was in, but really, unless she examined it, she was just speculating. Lana seriously doubted that Andrew would let her look at it.

She needed to just let it go.

He didn't want to talk about it so she wasn't going to push. To keep the peace, she would keep quiet about it, although she didn't want to.

Lana got up and had a shower. She found her overnight suitcase in the luxurious dressing room and changed into some comfortable clothes. Instead of heading back to the bed, which she was trying to ignore, she went to the sitting area of the suite and settled down on the couch to watch some television.

She didn't want to think about what had happened in that bed.

She was glad that it had happened, but now it was going to be awkward between the two of them. Which she didn't want, so she was going to make sure that there wouldn't be too much awkwardness between them as they had to live together and work together.

To the rest of the world they had to appear the loving and happy couple.

The door opened and he walked in, his hands in his pockets, and he looked as if he'd calmed down.

"Lana, I want to apologize," he said. "I didn't mean to storm out again. I just had to get my head together. I'm not used to people being a part of my life. I'm used to being alone."

"It's fine." Even though her father and Jack were always around, Lana understood where he was coming from. She spent a lot of her life alone. She didn't share much with anyone. She liked to keep parts of her life private. "There's no need to apologize. We're both adults."

As long as it was just her then she wouldn't get hurt or disappointed. She could just live her life.

No, you can't. When have you ever done that?

"Right." He sounded shocked.

"Yes. Some things are just better kept to ourselves and I'm sorry for prying."

He nodded and then took a seat on the chair in the sitting room. "I'm not sorry for what happened between us. I hope you don't regret it."

"No, I don't. And I stand by what I said. There doesn't have to be anything else between us. We'll just go on as originally planned until you get your green card. That's it."

Only she wanted to ask him why he was keeping her out, but then if she started prying again then he would start prying into her hang-ups. And she didn't want that.

All she wanted to do was keep the peace for the next year.

"Thanks, that's what I was hoping for." He looked as if he was going to say something more; instead he just said, "Thank you for being so understanding."

"Well, I want the same thing. I just want this year to be as peaceful as possible. We'll figure out a routine to work and live together. One that will let outsiders think we're having a happy marriage."

"We never really did talk about the end, did we?"

The question caught her off guard. "Other than divorce, I suppose we didn't."

"What're we going to say? And when, like right after I get the green card?"

"I don't think it should be right after you get the green card. That would be suspicious."

He nodded. "Good point."

"I'm not sure of timings but we'll have to come up with a plausible reason for us to end the marriage. My father stayed with my mother despite their unhappiness and I think if my mother hadn't have left he would still be with her now."

Andrew frowned. "That sounds miserable."

"Marriage is for life," Lana mimicked her father, making them both laugh and breaking the tension of the subject. "So, what do you think it should be?"

"Well, I want your father to still respect me. I do like my job, but then again he may not if we divorce."

The word *if* caught her off guard. "You mean *when,* right?"

"What?"

"You said *if* we divorce, but you meant *when,* right?"

A funny expression crossed his face. "Right. When."

"How about if you don't want kids and I do? If I tried to flip that he would try to convince me to have children."

"You don't want kids?" Andrew asked.

"Not really."

It was a lie, but it was a lie she'd always told herself because after David she'd never thought that she'd ever get married and have a chance to have them. She was also sure that she wouldn't make a good mother. She loved her career too much, just like her own mother had, and there was no way that she could ever walk away from a child, so she didn't want to risk it.

She didn't want to have a child, to protect both her heart and the child she'd never have. It was just easier to say it out loud that she didn't want them.

"I'm fine if you want to tell him that I don't want kids, because I don't. I've never been the paternal type."

Lana nodded. "Okay, so it all comes down to

when you get the green card; the timing of our divorce will be determined by that. Until that moment we'll just live in the same house, work at the same hospital and just try to live a civilized life."

Andrew nodded. "It sounds like a plan."

"Good." Only Lana didn't feel too good about that plan. Something gnawed at the back of her mind. Something unsettling. And she was exhausted. "I think I'll get some sleep."

"You take the bed and I'll just hang out here in the sitting room."

"Are you sure?"

"Positive. I'm not the one that did an extra-long surgery the night before our wedding. Go and have a good night."

"'Night." Lana left the sitting room and headed off to bed alone. Even though she'd been planning to go to bed alone since he'd walked away and even before they'd decided to sleep together, she really didn't want to be alone in the bed tonight.

She wanted to be with him, but after the talk they'd just had she knew that was next to impossible.

It would never happen. This marriage was just one of convenience.

There was an expiration date.

She'd spent her whole life alone and nothing was going to change now.

CHAPTER NINE

One month later

It's just a stomach bug. Or stress.

Stress was believable. Since her one stolen night of passion with Andrew, things had been awkward between them. He was rarely at her house, which was good, but when they did pass in the halls it was weird.

He'd seen her at her most vulnerable. It unnerved her that he'd seen her like that. Yet that night of passion had been incredible and, even though things were awkward between them, she couldn't get that night out of her head.

All she could think of was his hands on her body. His lips against hers and the pleasure she'd felt. It had been intoxicating.

Her stomach turned again as she crossed the ER floor and she knew then she couldn't hold it in any longer.

Lana ran to the bathroom, her hand over her

mouth, as fast as she could. People got out of her way in the emergency room, because all day Lana had been running to the bathroom, where she was sick. She just couldn't keep anything down. Smells that had never bothered her before, she could no longer stand.

The thing was, she had no fever but she was hot and sweaty. She had a feeling she knew exactly what it was, but she hadn't had the time yet to confirm it. And, frankly, she was too terrified by the prospect.

"Dr. Haole, I think you should go home," Clarissa, the charge nurse, said as she knelt down next to her, holding back her hair and then passing her a cool wet towel.

"I'm not sick," Lana tried to explain, but she sighed when she held the towel on her forehead. "I'm under the weather, but not sick."

Clarissa grinned at her. "I know."

Lana grabbed some toilet paper and wiped her mouth, the feeling of nausea subsiding. She leaned her head against her hand and sighed. "Thanks for holding my hair."

"You're welcome," Clarissa said. "I think you need to page your husband and do a test."

Lana closed her eyes and took a deep breath

and then looked at Clarissa, who had been a charge nurse for as long as Lana could remember. She was one of the only nurses who didn't think she was cold-hearted, who looked at her as a skilled surgeon and not the chief's daughter. "I can't be."

Clarissa just shook her head. "Doctors can be so stubborn and obtuse sometimes."

Lana took another deep breath, because she'd suspected it a couple of days ago when her cycle didn't start—and it was never late.

He wore a condom.

Of course, those were not infallible.

Great. Now how am I going to get an easy divorce?

"You might not be," Clarissa said, interrupting her thoughts. "It could be stress or a stomach bug. Still, it's better to be tested. You were married last month."

"Right, can you page Andrew for me?" Lana asked. "I have to clean up."

Clarissa nodded. "Sure. Should I page him to the ER or to your office?"

"The ER is fine. Send him to exam room five. I'll be waiting with a lab kit. He can draw my blood."

Clarissa nodded and got up, shutting the bathroom door behind her.

Oh, God.

There was no way they would be able to convince her father that divorce would be the right thing if she was pregnant. And terminating this pregnancy was something Lana didn't want to do either. This was her mistake and she stood by her mistakes.

Something her father had taught her to do.

I can't be pregnant.

A baby was not in the plans and she didn't know how Andrew was going to take it. Ever since their one night together, things had been awkward.

No, I can't be pregnant.

Of course it all made sense. Karma was such a pain in the butt. She got up from where she'd been kneeling over the toilet bowl. She flushed and then cleaned herself up. When she finally made her way down to exam room five she was thankful that she didn't get another wave of nausea. It had been the strong smells that wafted out of the emergency room, mixed with the disinfectant that had set her off. Now, as she navigated the hallway through the ER toward the exam room, she breathed through her mouth so that she could hold it together.

When she opened the door she saw that Andrew was in there, waiting for her. When he looked at her he wrinkled his nose.

"Whoa, are you okay?"

Andrew had been pretty scarce since their wedding night. Work kept her busy and when Andrew wasn't at the hospital he was out at the beach with Jack and his other clients, training them for the World Surfing Championship that was coming up.

Andrew had been oblivious to the last several mornings where she'd run to the bathroom to be sick.

Which was probably a good thing. Things between them were strained enough.

"I don't know," she said as she took a seat, because she was dizzy and the room was spinning. "I need you to run a test for me."

"Sure. What kind of test?"

"A blood test that's looking for levels of human chorionic gonadotropin in my blood."

"Human chorionic..." Then his eyes widened, the blood draining from his face, and he had to push his glasses back up. “Are you asking me to give you a pregnancy test?”

The words came out like a shout and Lana had to hush him and then hissed, “I don’t think the patients in the next pod heard you.”

Andrew ran his hand through his blond hair, his eyes wide behind his black-rimmed glasses. “Sorry, it’s just… I thought we used protection.”

“It’s not infallible. You know that. You’re a doctor.”

“So, you’re late?”

“No, I’m right on time,” she snapped. Then she scrubbed a hand over her face. “I’m sorry. I just haven’t been feeling well the last few mornings. It could be a stomach bug.”

Andrew’s mouth still hung open in disbelief. “Right, okay. Well, I’ll draw the blood and get it off to the lab.”

“Thank you. If word gets out to my father that I am, he’s going to make me stay at home barefoot and pregnant to raise his grandchild,” she muttered.

Andrew frowned. “Well, fathers can take paternity leave.”

Her heart swelled at the thought of him taking time off for their baby, which she wasn’t even sure existed at this point, but then she recalled the conversation that they'd had on their wedding night. He didn't want kids. He didn't want to be tied down.

That was what he'd told her.

And now she was probably pregnant. Only he didn't look too thrilled at the prospect of paternity leave and she felt guilty.

"If I am pregnant you don't… I can raise the baby." She was used to shouldering the burden of responsibility.

Andrew didn't say anything. "Let's not jump the gun."

"You said you didn't want kids."

"I don't." He pulled on surgical gloves as Lana peeled off her white lab coat. She was wearing scrubs so she didn't have to roll up her sleeves. He put a cuff around her arm and then swabbed her arm. "You'll feel a small pinch."

Lana rolled her eyes and he took a blood sample. Once he was done he pressed a cotton ball to her arm and then labelled the test tube.

"We'll figure it out," Andrew said, but she could hear the worry in his voice and the fear. "It could still be something else. Like rotavirus or something."

"Fingers crossed for food poisoning then?" she teased.

He smiled, but it was forced. She could see that he was just as worried as she was. And he wasn't making eye contact with her. Still as awkward since the night they'd slept together.

"I'll take this to the lab. Just sit tight. I don't think you should be out on duty right now, especially if you're vomiting everywhere."

"Agreed."

"I'll be back as soon as I can." Andrew left the exam room.

Lana lay back against the exam table and stared up at the ceiling. It was the first time she'd ever hoped that it was nothing more than a virus because it would make the separation from Andrew so much easier in a year, but deep down she really did want a baby.

It would cramp her career and it would make it more complicated for Andrew to leave cleanly, but she wasn't going to force him to stay if he didn't want to be a father. However, she was going to be the best mother she possibly knew how to be.

At least this child would love her unconditionedally. She didn't have to be anything other than a loving parent with this baby.

She could do this.

Maybe.

There were things she'd do differently—and she'd never leave.

You don't know that. Your mother left.

And that thought scared her to her core.

Andrew was pacing outside the lab. He was waiting for the results. He didn't say who the test was for. He just called the patient Jane Doe and made up an elaborate tale about how a patient needed an X-ray for a broken shin but wasn't sure if she was pregnant or not. So he needed a rush on the result.

The lab assistant bought it and now all Andrew could do was wait.

He'd never wanted to be a father. That was what he always told himself. How could he be a good father when he didn't have a good example to emulate?

Meghan liked you well enough.

The memory of his baby sister punched him hard in the gut. He hadn't thought about her in so long. She was always in the back of his mind, but since he'd married Lana memories of her came bubbling up everywhere. Good times and the night where he'd lost her.

And he didn't like it much, because it was a loss of control for him. Control he'd worked so hard for. It got him through the days, months and years. It was how he lived with himself.

"You're worthless! You've always been selfish, Andrew. Always!"

His father's words still echoed in his mind. It played on repeat, which was why he deserved everything he got. The loss of his career, both as a surgeon and a surfer, being alone—that was what he deserved. If only he had seen that moose before it was too late. Or reacted differently, faster…

"Dr. Tremblay, your patient's results are in."

Andrew spun around and thanked the lab technician. He didn't want to open the results without Lana present, but then if it was the news he wasn't looking for, if she was pregnant, he would have to be prepared.

Then she'd know you looked before her and she'd kick your butt.

He stared down at the report but he couldn't bring himself to look at it without her. So he headed back to the exam room where Lana was still waiting. She was staring up at the ceiling and when he entered the room she sat up slowly.

He could tell the simple action made her dizzy. *That's not a good sign.*

"Well?" she asked.

"I thought we'd look at it together." He handed her the paper. "You open it and we'll both read it." He girded himself for the prospect.

She nodded and took the paper from him. She unfolded it and he was hit with the whammy the same moment that she was.

Iolana was pregnant.

"Oh, my God," she whispered. "We were so careful."

"Yeah, well, as you said, condoms are not without fault." He raked a hand through his hair.

What am I going to do now?

This was all his fault. He'd ruined another life.

"I'm sorry, Lana. I know you didn't want kids either."

"Well, we have one." She bit her lip. "I'm not going to get rid of it, so that's not a suggestion I would even entertain, unless something medically came up."

"I can respect that. So what do we do?" Deep

down he wanted her to tell him to leave. To be angry at him so he could walk away. It would be better for the kid. He couldn't be a father. He didn't know how to be. His own father was terrible, he wouldn't do that to a kid, but then another part of him didn't want to leave her. He had to stay with Lana. It was the right thing to do.

"I can raise this baby on my own. Nothing has to change."

"Like hell nothing has to change," Andrew snapped. "That's my kid in there too."

"I am aware," she said. "We don't have to stay married to raise a kid. You're trying to get your green card to stay in the States, yes?"

"Yes."

Or he wouldn't have gone through all of this to try and stay.

"So we can co-parent this kid and not be married. People do it all the time."

"Yeah, but what about the reasons for our divorce? That I didn't want kids but you did? Your father is going to be none too happy."

"I know," Lana sighed. "Well, he'll be happy about the grandchild and that I'm becoming a mother."

That was said with contention and Andrew

couldn't help but chuckle. "Your dad is a bit of a dinosaur that way, isn't he?"

"He's old-fashioned."

"Lana, there's old-fashioned and then there's prehistoric!" They both laughed at that and then he took her hand and squeezed it to give her a sense of reassurance he wasn't feeling. "We'll figure it out."

"I know, but I just wanted you to know that I can handle this on my own. I don't want you to feel pressured, especially with the World Championships coming up." She was throwing up a wall. She was obviously just as scared as him.

Or she doesn't want you because you're worthless.

Andrew nodded. "Thanks. So what happens next?"

"I'll make an appointment with my OB/GYN. I just hope my dad doesn't get wind of this yet."

"Do you want me to come to that appointment?"

"If you want, but again, training Jack is your first priority. I mean, this is why we did this whole thing." She slid off the exam table. "I'm going to make my appointment and then finish my rounds, but preferably away from the emergency room so I don't have to continue breathing out of my mouth."

"What?" Andrew asked, confused.

She grinned. "The smells down here are getting to me."

"Ah, gotcha."

There was so much he didn't know about pregnancy. He knew the biology of it. He'd delivered a baby, but obstetrics hadn't been one of his best or favorite subjects during residency. He'd done his rotation and left it behind to study orthopedics. So he didn't know all the quirks, what set women off for morning sickness, but he had a feeling he was going to learn it fast enough. And it scared the hell out of him.

"I'm done for the day so I'm going to head down to the beach. Jack is waiting," he said. "When you get off you should come. The fresh air will help."

She nodded. "Yeah, that would be nice."

An awkward silence fell between them.

"Good. I'll see you later." And then, without thinking, he kissed her on the top of the head, catching them both off guard.

He had to put some distance between him and

Lana, but he also was going to do right by his baby. Even if that meant leaving in the end.

When Lana got home the first thing she did was shower, because she needed to wash the hospital off herself. Once she'd showered, she tied back her hair and put on a comfortable sundress and her sandals and made her way down to the beach, where she knew that Jack and Andrew were training.

Andrew was standing in a long sleeve wetsuit. It was unbuttoned and off his shoulders and as she came up behind him she got a good look at his scar. The one she had felt under her hands as they'd made love, when she'd held him tight through her pleasure.

Definitely his shoulder had been fractured. The scar ran over his right shoulder and down his arm and she knew she'd felt the rough skin in the front of the shoulder and she couldn't help but wonder if his accident had something to do with an impaling, only it had gone right through the bone, muscle and tore the joints.

He was lucky he still had his arm.

When she came closer, he turned and saw her there. So he set down his board and pulled on his board suit to hide his scar. "Hey, I didn't think you were going to come."

"I said I would," she said.

"I saw your car pull up and you went straight into the house so I thought you were tired."

"I am, but really I just wanted a shower first." She turned and looked at the waves, where she could see Jack shredding the nar. He was just a small figure riding a large wave and then Andrew handed her binoculars.

"Take a look. Your brother has good form."

"Thanks." She held the binoculars up and could see Jack, so focused as he maneuvered the board with precision. Their father might have wanted Jack to go into surgery like him, but Jack was born to do this.

Weren't you? You liked doing this.

Only she didn't get a chance to do this very often, but she did like surfing. When their mother had left, Lana became responsible and tried her best to make her father happy. Even if it meant giving up her dreams of being a sports medicine doctor and her dreams of surfing on an international stage, like Jack was doing now.

"You have a dreamy expression on your face," Andrew said. "What're you thinking about?"

"Surfing, but I'm not sure if I'll be doing much of that in the coming months." She handed him back the binoculars.

"Well, then, you'd better get it in while you can," he suggested.

"What?"

"You can surf still. Come on, you can still do it. You were doing it a month ago."

"I'm pregnant," she argued.

"Yeah, but it's not like you're taking up a new sport that your body is not used to. Your body is used to riding the waves. Go get changed, grab your board and get out there."

"Only if you'll come with me."

Andrew frowned. "I can't ride the big waves."

"I'm not talking about the big waves, but we can body surf some of these small ones. Come on, I know you do that. I've seen you out here too."

He narrowed his eyes and then a smile broke across his face. "Fine. Go get changed and we'll hit the surf."

"Good." Lana hurried back to the house and quickly got changed into her two-piece and then her board suit. She tied her long hair up into a bun and then grabbed two small body boards. When she got back, Andrew was down at the shore.

She handed him a board. “Race you?”

“Race?”

“Go!” She didn’t wait as she ran out into the surf, the cold water soothing her hot skin. She was still sweating, so the water and the surf crashing over her was welcome. When the water was waist deep she lay down on her board and paddled out, angling herself to catch a small wave. Andrew was behind her; he was grinning as the wave crested behind them and they rode it together back to shore.

Andrew was tossed before they hit the shore. When he popped up out of the water, still clutching the board, he shouted, “You cheated.”

“No way. I won. That wave didn’t toss me.”

“I think your gods probably shine favor on their *wahinis* who are pregnant.”

“Well, then, if that’s the case I’ll take full advantage.” She waded over to him and pulled him up, where he was sulking in the shallows. “Come on, that attempt was pathetic. You need to try harder.”

“Fine.” Then he turned and raced through the water, not waiting for her this time. Lana laughed as he paddled out to the next wave. "You're falling behind, Haole. You need to keep up."

Lana just shook her head and waded out in the water.

For one brief moment she forgot she was pregnant, that this marriage wasn't going to last and that she was probably going to have to raise this child alone.

For one moment she was just Iolana, enjoying her time in the water like she always did. It just made it all the more sweet to share it with someone.

Even if that someone was only temporary.

CHAPTER TEN

THEY WERE LYING out on the sand, letting the late afternoon sun dry them. Lana's eyes were closed and Andrew was mesmerized by her. She was fantastic in the water…that he knew.

And the thing that amazed and terrified him the most was that she was carrying his child.

The panic sunk in again.

How can I be a father?

He'd never wanted kids. All his life, even before Meghan died, his father had told him how becoming a father had ruined his life. Andrew didn't have a normal childhood. He didn't know how he could be a good father when he'd had no role model at all.

So he was terrified at the prospect of being a father. Of trapping Lana, who didn't even want to marry him in the first place.

And he decided to change the subject so that he wouldn't have a mild panic attack on the beach.

"Have you ever thought about surfing professionally, like Jack?" he asked.

"Once, but my father is a formidable force. He told me there's no future in it."

"There's a women's league and there would be a definite spot for you. I would've trained you."

"*Would* being the operative word," she teased. "In about nine months I don't think I'll be able to stand on a board. Heck, in three months, when the championships are happening, I don't think my center of gravity will comply."

"Still, Jack was pressured into becoming a surgeon but he didn't. He went after his passion."

She shot him a strange look. "Surgery *is* my passion. I've always wanted to be a surgeon."

"Really?" he asked; he wasn't so sure he believed her. He believed she loved surgery, but he didn't really get the feeling that she wanted to be Chief of Surgery or Head of Orthopedics.

"Why is that so hard to believe?" she demanded.

"You just seem to come to surfing naturally. So many don't."

"Well, once I entertained being a sports medicine doctor for the American surfing team, but my father vetoed that. It was a silly idea. I mean, they weren't going to hire me straight out of my residency."

"It's not a silly idea; you could've done it. You seem to belong out there. And you'd know how to care for an injured surfer."

"I like surfing, but it's a hobby."

Andrew's father had always thought it was a waste too. The only one who had supported him was Meghan, so Lana's words were like a slap to the face. The sport had been his whole world, as had surgery, and both had been snatched away from him in an instant. It was hard to hear Lana being so dismissive of something he thought they shared a passion for.

That's what happens when you assume, Andrew.

"So your plan is to work at your father's hospital until what? When he retires and you become Chief?"

Her lips pursed together and her eyes flashed with annoyance; he'd pushed her a bit hard. "And what's wrong with that?"

"Nothing. I guess it's safe."

"There's nothing wrong with being safe."

"That's where we differ."

She cocked an eyebrow. “Do we now? You don’t seem the type. You’re not a risk-taker.”

Another slap to the face.

Before he could say anything else, Jack came jogging up the beach with his board under his arm. He was panting, but he had been out there for some time.

“I think that’s it for me tonight, Coach.” Then Jack saw his sister. “Hey, Lana, what’s got your bees in a bonnet?”

“Oh, nothing, just that your coach here knocked me up.”

Jack’s eyes flew open in rage and Andrew jumped to his feet as Jack threw a punch that missed.

“You got my sister pregnant?” Jack shouted.

“Jack, I can explain.”

“No, I don’t think you can!”

“We need to take this somewhere private.” Andrew turned to Lana. “This is your fault. If he blows it…”

“Come on, Keaka. He’s my husband. I’ll make you some dinner and we can talk about this in a calm, rational manner.” Lana grabbed her brother’s arm and started pushing him up the beach.

Andrew was relieved, but he had a feeling this

wasn't over. He picked up the discarded boards and followed his wife and brother-in-law up to the house. And laughed at the absurdity of it all.

After he'd got the boards wiped down and locked away, Lana had changed and had Jack sitting on the couch. He had changed as well, but he was obviously really annoyed as he glared at Andrew when he walked into the living room.

"Andrew," Jack said in a haughty tone. Lana just rolled her eyes and handed Jack a bottle of water, before taking a seat at the opposite end of the couch, tucking her long shapely legs under her.

"Listen, Jack, I didn't mean this to happen. Your sister is a beautiful…"

"Don't say it," Jack groaned and pinched the bridge of his nose. "This wasn't supposed to be a real marriage. You weren't supposed to touch my sister."

"Your sister had some say in it too, Keaka," Lana said, but it wasn't helping.

Jack glared at Lana. "Don't call me that."

"I'll call you Junior if you don't ease up on Andrew," Lana growled at Jack, just like a mother to a son rather than a sister to a brother.

"So now what?" Jack asked. "Are you telling me this marriage is for real now?"

A blush crept up into Lana's cheeks as their eyes met.

"No," Andrew said, guilt eating at him. "But I'll be there for your sister and help raise the baby."

"Oh, man. Dad is going to be pissed when you two call it quits after you have his grandchild."

"I know," Lana mumbled. "Accidents do happen."

"I don't want to know," Jack moaned again. "I feel like this is my fault, Lana."

"It's not your fault, Jack. Although the debt you owe me will be astronomical."

Jack groaned. "Lana, you're making me feel bad."

"Good," she said firmly.

Andrew chuckled as he saw that feisty spark of humor bubble back up in Lana. "Jack, I plan to do right by your sister and our baby."

Jack scrubbed his hand over his face. "Okay. I believe you. I'm sorry for taking a swing at you, Andrew."

"Hey, I would've done the same if it was my sister." He regretted the words the moment they tumbled past his lips. They both looked at him with curiosity and he didn't want to talk about Meghan. He quickly blurted out, "If I had a sister, that is."

Pathetic save.

It seemed to work. Which was good, because he didn't want to talk about his sister. That was private. No one needed to know that.

That's no way to honor your sister's memory. Burying her in your mind. Not remembering the life she led.

"Jack, you can't tell Dad that I'm pregnant," Lana said, breaking Andrew from his guilt-ridden thoughts. "You have to swear that you'll keep it secret. I'm not that far along and I'm not ready to tell him yet."

Jack rolled his eyes. "He'll find out, you know. He has spies everywhere."

"He's right," Andrew agreed. "I'm sure we'll get a call tonight when he gets home from the hospital, congratulating us."

"On that note, I have to go." Jack bent over and kissed the top of Lana's head. "See you, sis."

Andrew felt a pang of longing. The last time that he'd seen his sister alive, he'd kissed the top of Meghan's head just like that, before they'd got into the car to head for home after a late night movie. He'd promised to look after her, because they were both united against their anxiety-ridden mother and angry, abusive father. The movie had been an escape. He'd been away working as a surgeon in Vancouver for three years. He'd come home because Meghan had begged him to.

Meghan was all he had.

Then she was killed in a head-on collision with a moose.

There was nothing he could do to save her because he'd almost died that night too, but that didn't stop his father from blaming him for Meghan's death.

You're not responsible.

"Are you okay?" Lana asked.

"What?" Andrew asked, shaking the thoughts of his sister from his head again.

"Jack said he'd see you tomorrow and you didn't even acknowledge him. You just stared out into space. I thought you went into shock."

"Nah—" he rubbed the back of his neck "—I just zoned out, but I wasn't thinking of anything in particular."

"So why don't you tell me about your family?"

Andrew stared at her. Her dark eyes penetrated into his soul and, though he should walk away, he felt like talking to her about his family. For once, in a long time, he didn't want to keep it all to himself.

He wanted to talk to someone about it.

"What is there to tell?"

She cocked her head to one side. "Come on, Andrew. We're going to have a baby together. I know our marriage isn't exactly real, but shouldn't I at least know about my baby's family? I know you're Canadian, but I don't know where you're from. I don't know your parents' names. I really know nothing about you."

"I like to be a man of mystery." He raked his hands through his hair and then saw that stubborn expression of hers set in. "Fine. What do you want to know?"

He didn't know where to start with it all, but he had a feeling that once the gates were opened everything would come pouring out of him and he had to regain some control.

"Where were you born?"

"Actually, I was born in Algonquin Provincial Park."

"You were born in a park?" she asked in disbelief.

"My mother was driving home from Huntsville to my hometown of Whitney. The park is this huge nature reserve and the road that connects Huntsville to Whitney is about sixty kilometers. Or thirty-seven miles for you Americans." He winked and grinned.

She chuckled. "Thanks, but converting something into metric doesn't explain the birth in the park thing."

"She went into labor right smack dab in the middle of that road. I came pretty fast and all she could do was pull off at the parking lot to a hiking trail and give birth. Thankfully, there were lots of tourists up from Toronto to see the fall colors and there was a doctor on one of those tour buses."

"So you were born in the fall?"

He nodded. "And you were born when?"

"Winter. Though I've never seen snow. After high school I went to Stanford in California."

"I've seen lots of snow. Too much, really."

She smiled. A sweet smile which made his heart skip a beat. "I'm sure. So you have a mother. Any siblings?"

"I lied before. I did have a sister, but she died." He was surprised at himself for telling her that. No one knew that outside of Ontario.

Her expression softened. "I'm sorry."

Andrew braced himself, expecting her to ask why or how, but she didn't. And he was relieved. Inevitably, everyone that found out he had a sister always asked those questions and he just didn't want to discuss it.

"How about your father?"

"There's not much to say." He shrugged. "He wasn't very supportive. My parents are still alive, but I haven't been home in quite some time."

"So, surfing? Why surfing? If you grew up in northern Ontario there really aren't many places to surf there."

He laughed. "I went to medical school in Vancouver and picked it up there."

"Ah, well, that does explain it." Her stomach grumbled and she winced. "I suppose I should try and eat something, though I don't feel very hungry."

"How about some chicken soup?" Andrew got up and went into the kitchen, poking around her bare cupboards. "Uh, when was the last time you went shopping?"

"Me? Why do I have to always go shopping? Don't be sexist!" She was teasing him. "Honestly, I forgot."

"Let's go out to dinner." He scooped up his keys from the kitchen counter. "Whatever you think you can stomach and we'll go there."

"That sounds great." She stood up, but teetered a bit. He raced over and steadied her. He'd been avoiding her for a month and just touching her again, being near her, reminded him how she felt in his arms.

A longing set in. He missed her.

"Are you okay?"

"Just dizzy," she sighed. "I hate this. I have a knee replacement tomorrow afternoon. If I'm wobbling around like this, how am I going to stand for all those hours?"

"I'll go with you," he offered. It was the least he could do.

"You will?"

He nodded. "Yeah. I'll make sure you don't throw up into the patient's incision."

Lana was going to laugh, but instead her eyes widened, her complexion turned green and she pushed him away, running to the bathroom, where he was privy to some not so attractive sounds on the other side of that closed door.

Good job, Andrew. You had to mention vomiting and incisions.

After Lana got over her spate of nausea the only thing she wanted more than anything was an ice cream cone. So Andrew drove to the nearest ice cream truck, which was parked beside a beach not far from her home, and now she was sitting on a bench, enjoying the sunset and her chocolate-dipped soft ice cream cone.

She said it was heaven.

He was chalking this up to the first of many pregnancy cravings. He'd complained that ice cream wasn't a good dinner choice. There was no sense in complaining; she was growing his kid after all. It was the least he could do.

"I think after you go to sleep I'm going to order in a pizza. Ice cream is not a very filling dinner," Andrew complained again.

"Yes, but please wait until I go to bed. You order some weird stuff on your pizza and no, I don't want to talk about pizza right now unless you want to see this ice cream come back up."

He chuckled. "I thought that your perfect wedding had something to do with pizza?"

"And unicorns, but you don't see me talking about those," she warned.

"Okay, message received. Enjoy the dairy goodness." He didn't particularly like the cones, so his ice cream was in a tiny paper bowl. It was cookie dough, something he'd always liked as a kid. The ice cream was okay, but the company was better. Lana looked so relaxed, her long bronze legs stretched out but crossed at the ankles. Her hair was braided back and she seemed to be glowing in the waning sunlight.

"You're glowing, you know," he said in awe.

"What?" she asked in disbelief.

"Isn't that a pregnancy thing?"

She snorted. "Maybe because of the sweat."

Andrew chuckled. "You know, you're quite funny when you're not trying to be so serious all the time."

"So you've said." She grinned at him. "It's been a busy month."

He knew she'd been avoiding him too.

"It was a fast month since our wedding." And the moment he mentioned the wedding all he could think about was the wedding night. The wedding night that he'd never meant to let happen, but he was powerless when it came to her.

He wanted her. Even now. He tried not to think of her, but memories of when he'd taken her in his arms plagued him constantly. He could still taste her on his lips, feel the softness of her skin on his fingertips and he wanted those long legs he'd just been admiring wrapped around his hips.

They finished their ice cream in silence.

There was a bit of ice cream on her cheek; he reached out and wiped it away with his thumb. Her eyes widened as he touched her and, before he knew what he was doing, his hand was cupping her cheek and then slipped behind her head, pulling her close to kiss her.

Lana melted into him and she tasted like chocolate and vanilla. The familiar scent of coconut and the beach wrapping him in a heady memory of the first time he'd kissed her. He'd known then that once was never going to be enough. And dammit, he was right.

She touched his face as the kiss ended. "What was that for?"

He wanted to tell her—because he couldn't resist her, because he was falling for her, but he couldn't formulate the words because he didn't want to believe it. There really was no future, because once his green card was in he could move to California and pursue a job that was made for him. The one with the International Surfing Committee, where he'd be the lead sports medicine doctor. It had been the dream all along.

Lana belonged to Oahu. She would never leave.

And, even though she was carrying his baby, he knew that eventually he would have to leave them behind. It would be the best for both of them. He wasn't father material. He wasn't going to screw up a kid like his father did to him. Besides, he didn't deserve the happiness of a family.

Then you shouldn't be kissing her.

And he hated himself for doing that.

"I don't know what came over me. I'm sorry. It won't happen again." Then he put distance between them, but as he tried to slide away she held tight to him.

"Andrew, I think we should talk about it."

"There's nothing to talk about, Lana."

"Isn't there?" she asked, confused. "We can't keep falling into this trap."

"I know. I'm sorry it happened. I truly am."

She nodded, but her eyes filled with moisture, as if she was about to cry. "Damn, I don't know why I'm crying. I totally agree with you. Freaking hormones."

"Another pregnancy thing?"

She nodded. "I'm really sorry, Andrew. I do think you're right. We have separate lives to lead, after this is all said and done. We can co-parent this baby and not be together."

"Right." He hated himself for thinking that he would one day leave Oahu and that he'd be leaving her with this responsibility, but it was for the best.

Wasn't it?

"Come on, let's get you home." He stood and then helped her to her feet. "You have to get your rest if you're doing a knee replacement tomorrow afternoon."

"That sounds great. I'm exhausted." As they walked back to the car Lana's phone began to buzz. She pulled it out of her pocket and frowned.

"Who is it?" Andrew asked, but he had an idea.

"It's my dad."

Andrew sighed. "Sounds like he found out."

"Clarissa was the one holding my hair and suggested I get a test." She accepted the call. "Hi, Dad, what's up? What rumors? Oh, those. Yes, it's true. I'm pregnant."

The cat was out of the bag.

Lana continued to talk to her father and for a brief moment Andrew entertained the notion of calling his parents and letting them know that they were going to be grandparents, but what was the use? They wouldn't care. They would just tell him how Meghan was never going to have children and it was all his fault.

His parents wouldn't care that Lana was carrying his child. That he was going to be a father. Calling his parents wouldn't put to rest the ghosts of his past; it would just remind him why he'd always said he never wanted to be a father.

How could he be a good father when his only example had been his own father?

CHAPTER ELEVEN

LANA COULD FEEL the beads of sweat pooling on her forehead. Once her father had found out that she was carrying his grandchild and that she was suffering from extreme morning sickness his first suggestion was that she go on maternity leave.

Right away.

When Lana kicked that suggestion to the curb in a very delicate manner, which stressed her out, standing up to him, to her relief her father acquiesced but stipulated that she see Dr. Peters right away. He prescribed her Diclectin, a safe medicine to ease her morning sickness so she could continue as a surgeon. And it seemed to be working.

It didn't take away the exhaustion and standing in an orthopedic hazmat suit while she did the knee replacement surgery didn't help. It was stifling in the suit. And even though there was filtered air cycling through she felt as if she couldn't breathe.

Focus.

She wished someone could wipe the sweat from her brow, but at least she was almost done with the surgery. Then she could shower and rest.

Andrew stood across from her and was actually holding a retractor. She had never seen him hold a retractor since he'd been here. She had seen him operate once on a surgical video. Maybe he would come to miss the surgery and start to perform here. If she had him doing surgeries on her service then she could ease off just a bit.

The other surgeons on the orthopedic surgical rotation were her father when time allowed and Dr. Sims and Dr. Kay. Dr. Sims and Dr. Kay both had a full practice.

There was room for the world-renowned Dr. Tremblay who had disappeared from surgery to aid with hers.

No one knew why Andrew had stopped performing surgery, but she had inkling it had to do with the surgery done on his shoulder.

He glanced up at her through the visor of his own hazmat suit. "You okay, Lana?"

"Fine. Just tired." She turned back to her work

and tried to ignore the fact he was standing there. It was hard, but she didn't want him to give anything away. Though she was pretty positive that most people in this room knew that she was pregnant, given the way that gossip moved through this hospital, but she didn't want to blurt it out in case her surgical team didn't know.

She didn't want anyone to think that she was weak.

It was bad enough that her facade had been cracked when she'd married Andrew so quickly during a sunset ceremony on the beach. And the speculation that Dr. Iolana Haole maybe wasn't quite the Ice Queen was starting to spread around the hospital. There were also rumors of Andrew using her to secure a green card and she knew those rumors were initiated by David. The problem was they were true.

And she didn't like it.

How the heck was she going to eventually take over the hospital if people didn't respect her the way they used to? The respect she'd worked so hard to regain after David used her before publicly humiliating her. The thing that scared her was she didn't care at the moment. She was enjoying herself at work. She wasn't so tense, wasn't so lonely.

Maybe because you don't want to run the hospital when your father retires. Maybe because you want to leave Hawaii. See the world.

Of course, those dreams were dashed now that she was pregnant. She couldn't go traipsing all over the world with a baby in tow. She had to give their child stability. She needed a steady job to provide for their child. That was what her father had said when he'd constantly worked after her mother had left. He needed to provide for her and Jack by working. That was the right thing to do and she'd do the same.

Any thoughts she'd had of having an adventure were dashed and she really had no one else to blame but herself, because she hadn't taken the chance.

She'd let her father rule over her. Let her fears of the unknown do the same.

Others made the decisions about her life. Not her.

You made the decision to sleep with Andrew. You made the decision to keep this baby.

She snuck another glance at Andrew and his gaze met hers and the way his eyes crinkled behind the surgical mask and visor let her know that he was smiling at her. Then he nodded slightly, giving her that boost of confidence she liked.

Lana went back to work. She was almost done with the knee replacement. A couple more solid taps to put the new joint into place and the replacement knee was in position.

"Good work, Dr. Haole," Andrew said.

"Thanks." She continued her work, closing the small incisions of the minimally invasive procedure. Her father still preferred the larger incision, but she'd trained to do the less invasive surgery.

She finished closing and gave her instructions about antibiotics in the IV and blood thinners and decompression stockings to the residents so they could monitor the patient in Recovery. Once that was done she headed to the scrub room as quickly as she could to get out of the stifling hazmat suit.

As soon as the scrub room doors shut she pulled off the helmet and took a deep breath of antiseptic scrub room air. Her hair was plastered to the top of her head under her scrub cap. Andrew followed her into the room and pulled off his helmet.

"You're drenched in sweat."

"I know," Lana said. "These pregnancy symptoms are magnified. Surely I shouldn't be feeling this bad?"

"Maybe it's twins." It was meant as a joke, but then he spun around, his eyes wide, as the realization hit the both of them. "Oh, my God, do you think it's twins?"

"I don't know," Lana said, dumbfounded. "It could be. Twins run in my family. My mother was a twin. Oh, Lord. Two babies." A wave of nausea hit her.

"Don't jump to conclusions. It might not be; you just might not handle pregnancy well."

"Then why did you suggest twins in the first place?" she shrieked.

"I was reading that pregnancy book you had on the coffee table last night while I was eating pizza."

"Are you seriously trying to make me hurl?"

"Sorry." He winced.

"So what did you read?"

"That sometimes pregnancy symptoms in the first trimester are amplified if there's more than one fetus."

Oh, my God.

The thought of two babies just sent her head spinning.

"Your mother was a twin, you say. That's what you said, right?" Andrew asked.

And, just like that, the mention of her mother sent a douse of cold water over her. It reminded her that her own mother couldn't handle her or Jack. That she'd hated being trapped with Lana's father. She'd hated Oahu. She'd hated it all and felt that Dr. Keaka Haole had ruined her life.

So she'd left. And Lana had become head of the household and tried to keep it all together afterwards. "Yes. I think so anyways. I'm pretty sure, but I could be wrong."

"Can you call and ask her?"

"Did Jack not tell you about our mother?" Lana asked in disbelief.

"No, well, other than she left your father, but that was it."

Lana sighed and she could feel tears stinging her eyes. "She left when I was a kid and Jack was a baby. I haven't seen her since. She didn't want anything to do with us. So no, I can't call my mother."

A strange look crossed his face for a brief moment, as if he understood what she was saying, but how could he? His parents had never abandoned him. He wouldn't understand.

"I'm sorry. Why don't we go up to Obstetrics? I'm sure, seeing how you're Dr. Haole's daughter, that they'd be more than willing to do a sonogram on you. It'll put your mind at ease."

"Yours too," she said sarcastically.

"Yes, twins would be…complicated."

She almost wondered if he was going to say *the worst*, but didn't.

"They won't see much."

"They'll see enough to tell whether there're two in there."

"Okay." Andrew was right. She wanted to know. It would drive her crazy not to know. She needed to plan and prepare herself. Lana had already mentally prepared herself for one baby, but the thought of two was a bit mind-boggling.

They finished scrubbing out and then headed straight from the operating room floor up to Obstetrics.

Dr. Green wasn't busy and took them right in. Which was rare.

Lana climbed up on the exam table, the paper crinkling and sticking to her sweat-stained butt. Andrew was chuckling to himself.

“Are you still having nausea, Iolana?” Dr. Green asked.

“Not as much, at least not since I’ve been taking the medication, but…twins run in my family.”

Dr. Green didn’t blink an eye. “I’m aware. Your father told me when he first told me you were pregnant.”

“Why would he tell you that?” Lana asked.

“He was covering all his bases,” Dr. Green said nonchalantly. “You know how he is.”

“Can you just ease our minds and tell us if there’re two in there?” Andrew asked, interrupting. “Lana’s been having more pronounced symptoms. Isn’t that an indicator for the possibility of twins?”

Dr. Green didn’t bat an eye. They called her the bulldog of the obstetrics floor because she didn’t put up with any nonsense. Which was why Lana liked her so much.

“It can be, but usually measuring larger than your dates and the presence of two heartbeats is how we determine twins, but it’s too early to catch a heartbeat with my sonogram. You’re only five weeks in.”

"Can you measure me or give me a transvaginal ultrasound and see what's going on?"

"Lie back and I'll measure you first. Then I'll do the ultrasound and we'll hopefully relieve some of your anxiety. Anxiety won't help with the symptoms."

Lana lay back and lifted up her scrub top. Andrew took a seat at her head while Dr. Green pulled out her measuring tape and measured Lana.

"Well… I'll be…" Dr. Green whispered.

Lana's heart did a flip flop. "I'm measuring larger, aren't I?"

"Yes, slightly. It could be just a large baby. How much did you weigh at birth, Iolana?" Dr. Green asked as she recorded the measurement in Lana's file.

"I was five pounds seven ounces, but I was early."

"And you, Dr. Tremblay?" Dr. Green asked.

"Ten pounds."

Lana bolted upright. "You were ten pounds and your mother gave birth to you in the middle of a park on the side of the road?"

Andrew grinned and winked at her. "Yep. We're hardy stock up in the north."

Dr. Green was chuckling. “It could be a larger baby, but we’ll check if we can see how many are in there. I’ll be back in a moment, so if you could put on a gown and remove your pants and undergarments in prep that would be great.”

When Dr. Green left Lana groaned. She got up and grabbed a hospital gown out of the cupboard in the exam room.

“Should I stay and watch?” Andrew asked, looking uncomfortable.

“Yes, because if our kid is ten pounds I’m going to kill you,” she hissed half-jokingly, but also terrified of the thought of giving birth to a toddler-sized infant.

He laughed. “Promises, promises.”

Lana removed her clothes while his back was turned and put on the gown. She got up on the table and Dr. Green rolled in the machine. She got the wand ready and Andrew continued to look away while she placed it and then covered Lana up with a sheet.

“You can look now,” Lana said.

Andrew turned around and took a seat back by her head. Dr. Green fiddled with some dials and stared at the screen.

Lana held her breath as the doctor recorded

measurements and studied the monitor. What was she going to do with twins? It couldn't be twins.

"Well, your hunch was right, doctors." Dr. Green turned the monitor around. Lana stared at the grainy picture and, though they looked nothing more than a couple of peanuts in a sack, she saw what was just about to be confirmed.

"Twins," Lana whispered in disbelief.

"Yes, you're expecting twins, Dr. Haole. Congratulations."

"Oh, my God," Andrew whispered and now he was the one that was looking a bit pale as he covered his mouth with his hand and stared at the screen. "Oh, my God."

Lana lay back down as reality sunk in. Now she really was trapped. Two babies. She'd told Andrew that she could do this on her own, but now she wasn't so sure.

How the heck was she going to raise two kids on her own?

They hadn't said much to each other when they left Dr. Green's office. Or during the ride home. Now they were just sitting on the couch side by side, not saying a word. Lana felt as if at this moment she should probably buy a state lottery ticket or something.

First the condom broke.

Then twins?

"What're we going to do?" Andrew asked finally, breaking the silence that had descended upon them ever since they'd found out that there were two babies in there.

"I know," she whispered. "You know I still stand by what I said before. I can raise these babies on my own."

"Lana, see sense. This is going to be more difficult." Andrew cursed under his breath.

"I can handle a challenge," she snapped, annoyed with his swearing. It was obvious he was unhappy about it.

Aren't you?

She got up and walked into the kitchen. Grabbing a glass, she poured herself some ice-cold water.

She was used to challenges. Her whole life had been a challenge. She'd had to teach herself a lot of things when she was a kid because her mother hadn't been around. She was the one who negotiated peace between her father and Jack. And because of who her father was she always had to prove herself more in her professional field.

There were a lot of times people thought she was given more opportunities because of who her father was and that was not true. She'd constantly sacrificed and worked hard for everything.

Now, two babies. It was a challenge, but she could do it.

Couldn't she?

"I know you can handle a challenge, Lana, and I know that you could handle this on your own, but I'm not going to let you." He touched her face and she backed away from his touch. She couldn't let herself get attached to Andrew, not when he kept putting up walls between them.

Not when this marriage was just one of convenience and would be over as soon as he got his green card. And not when he obviously saw her and the babies as a burden.

She couldn't let herself fall for him. She couldn't risk her heart. When her mother left, she'd seen how crushed her father was. Lana had taken it upon herself to try and comfort her dad, to make him happy again, but she'd been naive.

Her father's heart was broken and as she got

older and understood that she knew that she would never, ever put her heart on the line like that.

Except she did and then David crushed it. She'd sworn she never would again and then she'd slept with Andrew. She was so weak. Her heart was totally on the line and now she was carrying his children. She'd have double the reminder of him when he left and she knew he was going to leave. Once he got what he wanted he'd leave.

She set the glass down on the counter. "I'm going for a swim."

"A swim? Where, in the ocean? It's night."

"No, the pool." She strode past him and down the stairs to her bedroom.

Andrew followed behind her. "Don't you think we should talk about this? I mean, this changes everything."

"I know that it does, but I can't think straight right now, Andrew. I need to swim." She turned around. "This is a lot to take in."

"I know."

"I'm going to have to leave work sooner than I'd like. You know that twins often deliver early."

He nodded. "Yeah, that's going to be hard on the department."

"Well, if you had surgical privileges you could take over for me."

Andrew frowned. "Don't start this again."

"Why not? You want me to talk about this pregnancy? Well, I want to talk about why you gave up your surgical privileges when you came here."

"I can't operate." There was deadly calm to his tone and she knew that she was pushing him to the brink again. "You need to stop pestering me about this, Lana. I just can't operate."

"I know, because you don't have privileges," she said a bit too sarcastically, but she was tired of not knowing why. He still had his surgical license and if he would just do surgeries again he could take her place while she had their babies.

She knew that he'd be good at it. He was a brilliant surgeon and she didn't know why he was giving it up. She didn't get it. He was willingly giving up surgery and in a few months she'd have no choice but to go on bed rest and walk away, but she'd come back. She wouldn't give up the only thing in her life that brought her joy.

There were a lot of dreams that she had given up over the years, but surgery was not and would never be one of them.

"No, it's because my arm was damaged in an

accident four years ago. My surgery was botched and I can't hold a scalpel. I lost everything that day, Lana. I regained what I could, but I can't operate. I can't. My hand shakes, my arm is in constant pain. I don't react anymore because I've learned to filter it out or maybe my nerves are dying. I'm not sure. I was impaled after the car I was driving collided with a moose. Impaled by a metal signpost. It smashed right through the windshield and into my shoulder. My shoulder was damaged and the surgery was done by an old school doctor up in northern Ontario. So, that's why I don't operate. It's not safe for anyone. I can't do it. I won't."

And before she could apologize for pushing him too hard he stormed away to his room and slammed the door.

Lana felt bad for pushing him.

She knew the shoulder pained him. She'd seen and felt the scars and knew that his shoulder had been damaged, but she couldn't believe that he couldn't operate any more. He was terrified because of what had happened.

Some scars ran deeper than the surface.

She knew that all too well.

CHAPTER TWELVE

ANDREW GAVE UP on tossing and turning for the night. He got dressed and then checked on Lana, who was sleeping soundly. It was four o'clock in the morning and, even though his shift didn't start for another four hours, he just couldn't sit here stewing about it.

He grabbed his wallet and keys and headed out to his car.

At first he didn't know where he was going to go, but after driving around aimlessly for about fifteen minutes he made his way to the hospital. He changed into his scrubs and lab coat, but the hospital was quiet for now and he wasn't on call.

Not many people knew that he was here.

Which was fine, because he didn't really want people to see him standing in front of the skills lab, staring at it with contempt and a bit of fear.

He glanced down at his arm and his shoulder pained him. He flexed his arm and it trembled. It had been four years since the accident, since the botched surgery. Since Meghan died, he'd been alone after that. His parents blamed him and had left him to recuperate alone.

You're not alone now.

Except that he was. He wasn't in a real marriage.

Still, he couldn't face this fear. The couple of times he'd been in the operating room with Lana had been terrifying, but he missed being there. He missed surgery. He might not be able to compete on an international scale with surfing again, but he could reclaim surgery. He could help Lana by being a surgeon again. It would take some of the burden off her.

You don't deserve this. Your arm was penance for your sister's death.

He swiped his identification and entered the skills lab. It was dark and quiet. Later it would be filled with interns and residents as they tried to hone their art, just like he'd done when he'd been in their shoes.

Andrew took a seat and pulled out a surgical tray. He stared at the instruments and pulled on his rubber gloves. His hands shook as he picked up the scalpel. He took a deep calming breath and held it over the prosthetic abdomen.

You got this.

And then it came flooding back to him. Even though it had been four years, he knew exactly what to do. What kind of pressure to apply and the incision came so easily. Then pins and needles shot down his arm and he cursed, slamming the scalpel down.

What am I doing? I can't do this.

"Who did your surgery?"

Andrew's head jerked up and he saw his father-in-law standing in the doorway, his arms crossed.

"Sir, what're you doing here so early?"

Keaka shut the skills lab door and took a seat across from Andrew. "I couldn't sleep. I was thinking about Lana's news. About how I'm going to be a grandfather to twins no less. And you couldn't sleep either, I see."

Andrew sighed. "Yeah, I thought… I don't know what I thought."

"When I first hired you on here I knew that in time you would try and return to surgery, but I didn't want to rush you. You're a brilliant sports medicine doctor and you've helped many of our patients. You're a valuable asset, Andrew, but you were an impressive surgeon."

"My arm is useless. It's like a dead weight. There's nerve damage."

Keaka nodded. "Who did your surgery?" he repeated.

"Dr. Wilbert Guzman in a small backwater hospital up in Canada."

"I don't know of him, or that hospital. I don't know the severity, but a simple laparoscopic arthroscopy might release the scar tissues, ease the inflammation of the nerves and help with that shaking. I could do the procedure later today if an arthroscopy is called for."

One voice inside him said, *Do it.* The other said it would never work. He was too damaged.

"And what about my rounds, my patients?"

"I can handle that for you and I'm sure Lana could pick up some slack. If a simple procedure is needed you'll only be off for a week at tops."

Andrew looked down at his shaking arm. He was tired of being afraid. Tired of living in the periphery of his life. If he could regain control of his arm and practice surgery again he would have something.

Maybe then his kids would look on him with a sense of pride, because he wasn't giving up any longer. He'd run for so long, hiding his shoulder damage like a shameful secret. He might not know how to be a father, but at least his kids wouldn't be ashamed of him the way he'd always been ashamed of his father.

"Okay. Let's do it," Andrew said.

Keaka grinned. "Good. Now, let's get you down for a CT scan and we'll get some imaging done of that shoulder. I would do an MRI but I assume there's hardware in that shoulder?"

Andrew nodded. "You're correct."

"Well, let's go then. Let's see what we have to work with, shall we?"

Keaka opened the door but Andrew stopped him. "I just want to say…whatever happens, thank you. I will take care of Lana and the babies. Whatever happens, they're my first priority."

Keaka smiled and clapped Andrew on the shoulder. "I know, son. If they weren't your first priority then I wouldn't have found you sitting here in the skills lab. You would still be hiding from the damage that was done."

"I suppose you're right."

"I know that I am. And I know there are rumors that you only married Lana for a green card, but now, with the babies and your agreeing to surgery, I know those rumors are unfounded. Now, let's get down to the CT scan before it's flooded with patients from the emergency room and residents."

Andrew nodded but his stomach was knotted, guilt eating at him as he shut the lab skills door.

Keaka was reaching out to him, willing to help him like a father, and Andrew was lying to him. And he was terrified about the outcome, but he had to try. There were thoughts replaying in his mind that this surgery wouldn't work. That his arm would be worse off, but if he didn't take this risk then he couldn't take the biggest risk of all—trying to prove to Lana that he was a worthy man.

That he would be a good father.

Though he seriously doubted he would be. He didn't deserve happiness. He was responsible for Meghan's death. Still, he wanted to try with her, even if it didn't work out in the end. He wanted to try.

When Lana woke up at six in the morning she was surprised to see that Andrew had left already. So she got ready and headed over to the hospital. When she walked into her office her secretary informed her that her father and Andrew were down at CT. Andrew was waiting for his CT and her father had booked an OR for Andrew for three in the afternoon; her father wanted her to bring in an overnight bag for her husband.

"What?" Lana asked in confusion.

"Just what I said. Dr. Haole wants you to bring an overnight bag for Andrew because he's scheduled to have an arthroscopy late this afternoon."

"They're in CT right now?" Lana asked.

Kelley, her administrative assistant, nodded. "Right now."

"Thanks, Kelley."

Lana made her way down to CT and found what room they were in. She could see her father and the technician discussing images that were coming on the screen and when she glanced into the room she saw Andrew with an IV attached, his damaged arm raised above his head and lying on a bed as he passed through the CT.

"Dad, what is going on?" Lana asked.

Her father and the technician turned around at the same time.

"Iolana, come see for yourself." Her father stepped aside so that Lana could get a good look at the screen.

And there she saw the details of Andrew's shoulder injury. What should've been a simple dislocation and repair to remove whatever had impaled him had been cut away instead, causing adhesions which pinched the nerves and were probably responsible for all his symptoms.

"I was worried that it might be a bit more complex and I would have to completely open up the shoulder, but I think a simple arthroscopy will take care of all his issues." Her father was grinning and Lana was dumbfounded.

"Did Andrew agree to this or did you coerce him?" she asked. Although she seriously doubted her father could coerce Andrew.

"Iolana, I don't coerce anyone."

Yeah, right.

She rolled her eyes, but her father didn't see that. "So, he's actually going to go through with it?"

"If it is minimally invasive, yes. Come on, let's go tell him." Her father headed into the room where Andrew was now out of the CT machine and sitting upright again, rolling his shoulder and a pained expression on his face.

When he saw her he didn't really make eye

contact with her. And it stung. He was still mad at her.

"Well?" Andrew asked her father instead. "What's the verdict?"

"Adhesions," her father said. "A simple arthroscopy will take care of it."

Andrew nodded and then looked at her. "Will you be okay if I do this?"

"Why would it affect me?" Lana asked, trying to be nonchalant instead of telling him *I told you so.*

"Iolana!" her father said in shock.

Andrew grinned. "No, she's right. It's my decision."

"Exactly," Lana said. "It's your decision, but I think you should let my father do the surgery. The adhesions are impinging on a nerve and the surgery will allow a release and improvement of the arm."

"After extensive physiotherapy to build up my strength again," Andrew added, not breaking the connection with her.

"Not so extensive, as an arthroscopy is minimally invasive," her father interjected. "Well, if you're giving approval, Andrew, I will get the operating room ready for this afternoon. We'll get you into a room to wait until your procedure."

When her father left she turned back to Andrew. "Are you sure?"

"Yes…no. Actually, I'm not sure this will work." Andrew then shrugged. "What do I have to lose?"

"I will help you any way that I can," she said.

"You don't have to. You have enough to worry about; I don't want to add any more stress to your plate. You don't need that."

"What would've been more stressful is you not telling me that you were having surgery and I found out after the fact." She sighed. "I'm sorry for pushing you."

Andrew chuckled and she knew she was forgiven. "You know that you can't be in the operating room, right?"

"Seriously, you're letting me know this? Am I not a surgeon here? I know the protocols."

"Yeah, you are, but sometimes surgeons and doctors can overstep their bounds when it comes to…" He trailed off and Lana couldn't help but wonder if he was going to say *loved one* or imply that they were family. Instead he rubbed the back of his neck. "They sometimes need a reminder."

"I understand," she said quietly. They might be having babies together, but there was no love; they weren't family. They were in a business arrangement.

The orderlies came in with a gurney. "Dr. Tremblay, we're here to take you to your room now."

"I can walk," Andrew said.

"Uh, what was that about doctors needing a reminder, Dr. Tremblay?" Lana teased. "Hospital policy. Get on that gurney and I'll come by and see you before your surgery."

"Yes, Doctor." Andrew winked and climbed onto the gurney while the orderlies got his IV bag. He waved as they wheeled him from the room.

Lana couldn't believe he was doing this. She was happy that he was doing it, but also a sense of terror hit her hard. The thought of Andrew in surgery, where something could happen to him, made her worry all of a sudden.

Don't think about it. He's in good hands with Dad.

Her father had done multiple arthroscopies for the same issue and they had all been successful. Next to her father, she was highly adept at them, but she couldn't perform the surgery on Andrew since they were married.

What she had to do today was bury herself in her work and not think about Andrew going under the knife. If she kept busy, the time would just fly by.

After she left the CT floor she headed straight for her rounds, making sure that all her surgical patients on her floor were comfortable and were healing well. And when that was finished she grabbed a quick bite to eat and then did a skills lab on arthroscopy with the residents with her father, who was looking for a keen resident who was interested in orthopedics to assist him in Andrew's surgery later today.

It didn't take long to pick the resident. Once that was decided she went back to her office to grab a few things before she headed up to the surgical floor. She might not be able to be in the operating room while Andrew was undergoing his surgery, but she was going to be in the gallery watching and she would be there when he woke up.

And she told herself over and over she was doing this because people would expect this from her as his wife, but she wasn't convinced, because it felt right to do that.

When did she go from pretending to be a wife to feeling like a wife?

You're not a real wife. Don't think like that.

"Ah, well, if it isn't the beautiful bride."

Lana groaned and turned around to see David standing behind her, smirking.

"Dr. Preston," she said through gritted teeth.

"Oh, come now, you're the blushing bride who is head over heels in love." He snorted in derision. "You couldn't marry me for a business arrangement, but you marry Dr. Tremblay for a green card."

"What're you talking about?" she snapped, though inside the butterflies in her stomach were having a field day.

"Oh, come on. You honestly expect me to believe it was love when I saw him chasing skirt around this hospital from day one."

Heat bloomed in her cheeks, but from rage. Not embarrassment. "No, you have the wrong person. That was you, David."

"He's using you, Lana."

"What does it matter to you?" she asked.

"I'm at least a surgeon still."

"I'm in love with Andrew, Dr. Preston."

He snorted and rolled his eyes. "Right."

"Andrew has never once cheated on me. Andrew is in love with me and if you're not up to date on hospital gossip, then I'll let you in on a little secret—Andrew and I are expecting twins."

David's mouth dropped open. It was apparent he hadn't heard and she was pleased for making his head spin. She had nothing left to say to him, so she turned on her heel and left him standing there, gawking.

Even though the only thing true in that statement was the fact she was carrying Andrew's babies, it felt good to give David a bit of a comeuppance. To stand up to him finally.

She headed back to her office and as she rounded the corner she saw Kelley was not at her desk, because she'd put her sign up that she'd be back in ten minutes, but there was a woman standing there waiting. She had her back to Lana. She was well dressed in a business suit and heels, her grey hair tied back in a neat bun, and the first thing that popped into Lana's mind was that she must be a drug rep and that she probably had a meeting she'd forgotten about.

Yet there was something about this woman

which tugged at the corners of her mind. A nagging sensation which was telling her that she should know this woman.

"Can I help you?" Lana asked cautiously.

The woman's spine stiffened and she turned round slowly.

The world began to spin for Lana as she stared into the familiar blue eyes of the woman she'd thought she would never see again.

"Hello, Iolana."

"Hello, Mother."

CHAPTER THIRTEEN

LANA'S PULSE WAS still thundering between her ears as she shut the door to her office. She had showed her mother in, because she really didn't want to be discussing anything with her estranged mother with the door open to a hallway of the hospital, where anyone could be listening. She didn't need any more rumors flying about.

Her mother's impromptu arrival today was the last thing that she needed.

Didn't she have enough to deal with? She didn't need a woman who had checked out of her life, given up her children, forced Lana into early adulthood, to suddenly appear.

And as she eyed up the woman who'd left her all the things she wanted to say to her remained locked away. There was so much she wanted to ask her, to tell her how she really felt about her abandonment.

Why did you leave Jack and me? Are you inherently selfish? How could you break Dad's heart?

Why didn't you love me?

Why wasn't I good enough?

Only, like always, she lost her voice.

"I suppose I should explain why I'm here."

"Does it matter?" Lana asked, crossing her arms; she found it hard to look her in the eyes. Jack had her eyes and it was eerie now to think about it.

"You're so like your father."

And that angered Lana. How would she know? She knew nothing about her.

"Why did you come back?" Lana asked.

"I wanted to talk to you."

"Then talk, because I really don't have much time. I have patients to see."

"How long will you give me?" her mother asked.

"Ten minutes." And that was ten minutes too long.

"I don't think that's an adequate amount of time to properly talk to you."

"Take it or leave it."

"Can we meet later for coffee perhaps?" her mother asked.

Lana was tempted, only because some part of her wanted to know the answers to all those questions that had plagued her, her whole life. Those questions which had crippled her self-esteem and made her doubt herself far too many times, but that part of her was small. The other part of her didn't want to get to know the woman who had abandoned her and Jack. The woman who'd broken her father's heart.

"No, I don't think so." Lana opened the door to her office.

Her mother sighed and moved toward the door. "Okay. I see then."

Lana shut the door behind her mother, her hands shaking.

Get a grip on yourself.

And she glanced at the clock on her wall and realized that it was after three and that Andrew was being taken down to the operating room and she wasn't there.

She checked herself in the mirror and made sure that she'd calmed down. Lana was relieved when she opened the door to her office and saw that her mother was nowhere to be seen. She'd taken her advice.

Lana made her way to the OR floor and took her place in a packed gallery. One of the residents offered to give up his seat in the front so she could sit in the front row, but Lana wouldn't let him get up.

"You need to watch this, Fergus. More than I do."

Lana preferred to stand anyways.

Her heart was hammering as she saw Andrew under general anesthesia. Those beautiful blue eyes taped shut, a tube down his throat and her father making the incisions to drop the instruments into the shoulder.

Oh, God.

A rush of emotion washed over her and she closed her eyes to pray. She prayed this worked, because she was worried that if it didn't he'd blame her and she didn't want that.

"Did you know that Dr. Tremblay applied to the ISC?" one resident said to another.

"What is the ISC?"

"The International Surfing Commonwealth. If he gets in there he'll be leaving to go to California. It's a high profile job and he'd be working with some of the best athletes in the country. That's why he's finally getting his shoulder fixed properly. He won't get the job if he can't do surgery. They want surgeons and the surgeon who invented the Tremblay method would be an asset."

Lana's heart sank. She didn't know why it surprised her.

Of course Andrew would've applied to the International Surfing Commonwealth. He'd mentioned that as one of his goals, one of his reasons for staying in the United States and getting his green card. Only she hadn't known that he'd actually gone and applied for the job. It was just the confirmation of the fact that their time together really was limited and that she would be alone with these babies.

She would be all they had.

And she would have to be enough.

When Andrew woke up from his surgery he was in some pain, but pain that he was used to, so it didn't faze him too much. Then he recalled that he'd had surgery on his shoulder and his eyes popped open, but since he didn't have his contacts in or his glasses on the room was fuzzy.

"Here," Lana said from the haze, slipping his glasses on. He was relieved to see her smiling face, which surprised him.

"Thanks," he whispered, his throat bothering him from the general anesthesia tube.

"No problem."

"How did it go?"

"It went smoothly. Dad removed the adhesions and as soon as the nurses in the recovery room feel that you can go home I'll take you there and make sure you're comfortable."

"You don't have to do that," he said. "I can take care of myself."

"Of course I do. I can't let you recover on your own."

"I should be taking care of you."

"Andrew, I'm only five weeks along. It's okay. Let me do this for you. Later, when I'm as big as a house and probably very grumpy, you can make it up to me."

He sighed, because it hurt to laugh. He didn't want her staying because he didn't want to put her out, but he was relieved she was there. He was relieved that he didn't have to do this alone.

It took him a couple of hours to shake the effects of the anesthesia, but soon the world became clearer and Lana never left his side. Finally her father came in and he was smiling.

"You did excellently. You need to rest that arm

for at least ten days and then you can start to work it again—gently at first, though."

"Thank you, Dr. Haole," he said.

"I think you can take him home now, Lana." He nodded and then squeezed Lana's shoulder.

"Well, let's get the IV out of you and get you home where you can rest."

"That sounds good." And it did. It had surprised him when she'd said *home*. He didn't have a home, or hadn't had a home in so long, that it felt weird when she referred to the place he was temporarily living as home, but he wasn't going to argue that fact.

He needed some rest.

The nurse removed his IV and helped him get dressed. And then an orderly brought a wheelchair. He was going to argue about being wheeled out, but Lana fixed him with a gaze that brooked no argument. So Andrew let the orderly wheel him out to Lana's car, which was waiting in the front loop outside the hospital.

The orderly helped him into the car and Andrew dozed during the short drive home. When Lana parked at her house Jack was waiting and he helped Andrew inside to the bedroom upstairs, where he was tucked into bed.

"Thanks, Jack," Andrew said.

"No problem, Coach. Get some rest."

"Thanks, Jack." Lana kissed her brother on the cheek.

"Are you going to be okay, Lana, or do you want me to stay?" Jack asked.

"I think I can take care of Andrew. Go home. I'll talk to you later."

"Okay, 'night."

Lana turned back to Andrew and pulled out a thermometer.

"What are you doing with that?" he asked suspiciously.

"I was just going to ask you to roll over and drop your drawers." There was a twinkle of humor in her eyes as she stuck the thermometer in his ear. "I'm taking your temperature to watch for a post-operative fever, you dolt."

"God, you're a pain." He winced as it chimed in his ear. "Well?"

"No fever. Which is good." She set the thermometer down. "Anything you need?"

"No." Lana got up to leave but he reached out with his good arm and held her back. "Don't go." It surprised him, but he didn't want to be alone. He was tired of being alone.

She sat back down. “Are you okay?”

“I just want you to sit here for a while. Last time I had a surgery I was alone when I recovered. There was no one caring for me and… It was scary. So just sit with me until I drift off.”

“Okay,” she whispered softly.

“You can lie next to me.”

“Okay.” She rounded the bed and cuddled up next to him. “So why were you alone last time? Didn’t your family help you?”

“No,” he said. “I haven’t spoken to my parents since I was in the accident.”

“Why?”

And maybe it was the painkillers, or because he was tired of holding it all in and needed to talk to someone about it. “Because my father is a drunk and my mother was just a pawn for him. They blamed me for my sister’s death, you see.”

“They blamed you?” she asked, confused.

“She was in the car with me when we hit the moose. I know it wasn’t really my fault, but they blamed me. Or Dad did and Mom just went along with him. They disowned me and I haven’t been home in a very long time. I took the blame, because I am to blame. Maybe my reactions weren’t fast enough. Maybe I could have steered a different way. Maybe I should have been concentrating more."

"I'm sorry," she said. "I'm sorry you had to go through that last surgery alone. I'm sorry you lost your sister, but I don't think you're to blame, Andrew. It was a tragic accident. You don't have to be alone this time either. I'm here for you."

"I appreciate it."

"Speaking of parents, I had an unexpected visitor today."

"Oh, yes?" he asked, intrigued. "Who?"

"My mother."

Now he was surprised. "What did she want?"

"I don't know. I didn't really talk to her. It was a shock to see her."

He was going to ask more questions, but he was getting tired again. The painkillers were taking effect. "Does Jack know?"

"No, but I will tell him. He has the right to know and make up his own mind. He was very young when she left; he doesn't remember her."

"That's good," he mumbled and then he slouched over and laid his head on Lana's shoulder. The scent of her shampoo and the warmth from her body lulled him off to sleep. And, for the first time in a long time, he felt as if he was safe.

As if he was home.

"Would you stop fussing over me? I'm fine."

Lana crossed her arms. Andrew had been off for the ten days since his successful arthroscopic procedure. While she'd been at work she'd made sure that Jack came and looked after him. About day three was when Andrew started resisting help and wanted to get back to doing everyday things.

And not once did he complain about his shoulder.

There was tenderness as it healed, but the pained expressions from the constant ache he'd felt wasn't there. At least as far as she could tell, observing him.

"Today is your last day off; you get assessed and then tomorrow you can go back to work and start your rehabilitation. Until then, you should take it easy."

Andrew shot her a look of derision. "My incisions have healed well. They weren't even stitched up. The incisions were minor."

She rolled her eyes. One thing she'd never believed was that old saying that stated that doctors made the worst patients, but in Andrew's case it was true.

"Sit down and eat your breakfast." She set down a plate of fruit and scrambled eggs in front of him.

He cocked an eyebrow and looked at it in disbelief. "You cooked this?"

"Yeah, sure. I know how to scramble an egg."

"Since when? When you made me breakfast a couple of days ago the toast was black and I swear I ate eggshell."

Lana rolled her eyes. "Fine, I ordered in."

"Whew, then I can eat it," he teased.

She picked up a tea towel and tossed it at his head. "I'm so done looking after you!"

"Sit down and eat," he said. "You need to eat more than I do."

Lana took a seat at the table and took a bite of fruit. She was glad the Diclectin was helping her keep her food down and her morning sickness was now subsiding as she approached week seven of her pregnancy.

"How is your arm feeling today?" she asked.

"It's good," he said in slight disbelief as he flexed his fist. "Stiff, but good. I'd take the stiffness and the healing pain over the electric shock of an impinged nerve any day."

"I bet." She pushed the scrambled eggs around on her plate. "Have you called your parents?"

His eyes widened. "Uh, didn't I tell you about my parents? They disowned me."

"I thought you would tell them about the babies."

"And did you tell your mother about the babies?" he countered.

"Good point." She took a sip of the orange juice, though what she really wanted was coffee. "I did, however, talk to Jack about it. He hadn't been checking his messages. Apparently she called him before she went to the hospital to try and find us."

"How did that go?"

"Surprisingly well. He wants to meet with her and I told him that he could contact her."

"Do you know what she wants?"

"No, and I don't need to know." She glanced at the clock on the wall. "You need to finish up. We have an appointment to get you cleared for surgery."

"Right." He didn't seem to be enthused about it.

"It'll be great. You'll get cleared, I'm sure."

"You seem so sure." He smiled at her. "I like your enthusiasm. It's a refreshing change from the Dr. Iolana Haole, Ice Queen."

She frowned. "Ha-ha. I'm still an ice queen."

"Is that a fact?"

"My residents still fear me." She picked up her plate and put it in the dishwasher. "Are you done? Come on, let's go."

"Fine." He got up and scraped his plate into the garbage disposal and then put it into the dishwasher. He was standing so close to her and for one minute she reveled in the feeling of domestic bliss. Which scared her. She didn't want that. She didn't want to trap him if he was offered an ISC position, the way she'd been trapped when her mother left.

She moved away and grabbed her purse. "Come on, you don't want to be late for my father. If you think that I'm an ice queen then you haven't had to deal with the tyrant too much."

"That's because he likes me."

Lana rolled her eyes and opened the door. Andrew was still chuckling to himself as he climbed into her car and they took the short drive to the hospital.

When they entered the hospital, the staff who

knew that Andrew had undergone the surgery welcomed him back. He seemed uncomfortable with the well wishes and she knew that he was nervous about what the assessment would say.

Without thinking, she took his hand but he didn't try to pull it away. Instead he squeezed her hand.

"If the assessment goes well and they clear me for work I think I'll spend the rest of the day in the skills lab," he said.

"That sounds like a good plan," she said.

"I'm not returning to surgery until I'm fully confident that my hand doesn't shake."

"I get that, but really there's only so much a skills lab can prepare you for. You won't really know your abilities until you get back into the OR and work on a patient."

"I'm not risking a patient's life," he snapped.

"I didn't say that, Andrew."

He scrubbed his hand over his face. "Of course. I'm sorry, I'm just nervous about this."

"I get it." She opened the door to her father's office. "It'll be okay. You got this."

A strange expression crossed his face when she said that. Words that he'd said to her time and time again. He let go of her hand then and headed into her father's office.

Lana sighed and followed.

She wished she could do more to help him. She wished she could help heal the emotional rift between his parents and him.

You're one to talk.

The thought caught her off guard and she shook it out of her head.

The door opened and Andrew looked up from where he'd been working on his skills for a few hours, ever since he was given the all-clear to go back into surgical rotation.

He'd been working and his arm was behaving. There was pain, but it was good pain. Now he understood the difference.

Still he was not satisfied.

I can't go back into an operating room.

"You've been in here a while," Lana said and in her hand she was holding a bag of takeout food, which smelled delicious. "Hungry?"

"Yes. Starving."

She shut the door and brought the food over to a table that wasn't cluttered. "How is it going?"

"It's going." He reached into the bag and pulled out a box of Chinese food.

"Don't push yourself too hard. You're still healing."

"Yes, Doctor," he teased. "I promise I've been good."

"Good."

He dug into the food. "Thank you for bringing me dinner."

"Well, I wanted to go home, but I didn't want to abandon you at the hospital so I brought you food as a bribe to get you to leave."

"I can take a cab. It's fine. You need your rest."

She shrugged her shoulders. "I've gotten used to you being around and sleeping beside you."

Fire flooded through his veins. In his worry over his arm and whether he'd be able to operate again he'd forgotten that they'd been sharing a bed. It had been nice, but it had to end. He didn't want to lead her on. To hurt her.

But you have kids together. That can't be erased.

And the memory of how they'd conceived their twins came flooding back to him. Every night she'd been by his side, yet he had blocked out the fact that for the last ten days Lana had been sleeping next to him.

Usually curled up right beside him.

That first night when he'd come home after surgery he hadn't wanted her to leave him. He'd wanted her to stay until he fell asleep and she had, but he'd woken up beside her. Every night they went to bed together, her arm over his chest as he slept on his back.

It had been the best ten days of sleep he'd ever had, but he hadn't put much thought into it until now, because it had always felt right. It was scary.

"Well, it's been nice, but I think we should probably go back to the way things were."

"You're right," she said quietly and he knew then that he'd hurt her. It hurt him too.

She finished her dinner. "Will you be at the obstetrician appointment tomorrow?"

"I'll try to be. What time is it?"

"Seven. Dr. Green is staying late to accommodate the both of us."

"I'll try to be there, but I do have rounds. I may not go into the OR yet, but I do have my regular patients to look after." Then he swallowed the lump that was forming in his throat. "Thank you for taking care of my patients, by the way. I… You've done so much for me."

"Well," she said softly, not looking at him. "That's what friends are for."

Hearing her refer to them as friends stung. Why did he think that they were something more?

They didn't say anything else to each other as they finished their dinner, cleaned up the skills lab and then drove home together. Once they got home Lana said a quick goodnight and headed back down to her bedroom downstairs and Andrew headed upstairs.

The house was silent, emptier somehow.

This is for the best.

He got out of his clothes and had a quick, cold shower, trying to chase away thoughts of her and cool down the fire which burned him. Of course, since this was a different kind of fire, the cold shower was doing absolutely nothing to help him.

He turned off the faucet and opened the windows. The wind was coming off the ocean and the palm trees were moving quickly. There was a storm blowing in. He could hear the distant rumblings and, as he stood there, he could see the flash of lightning.

Footfall behind him caused him to turn around.

Lana was standing in the doorway in her nightgown, her hair loose and spilling over her shoulders. She was mesmerizing and all he wanted to do was take her in his arms again.

Just once more.

"Lana?"

"I couldn't sleep. I know that it's better this way, sleeping separately, but can I sleep beside you tonight?"

Andrew didn't answer her. Instead he closed the gap between the two of them, cupping her face in his hands and kissing her the way he'd wanted to since their wedding night. If his shoulder wasn't newly repaired he would've picked her up in his arms and carried her to bed, but the bed wasn't far and she seemed to have the same idea as him because she led him over to it. He pressed her against the mattress, this time not worrying about the need for protection.

All he had to think about was how good she felt in his arms.

Mine.

He braced his weight on his good shoulder, his other arm moving between her legs, causing a groan to bubble up in her throat. One that drove him wild with need. His blood thundering through his body, like the thunder rolling outside.

Andrew couldn't get enough of her. He burned for her. She was his drug and he needed her and it terrified him how much he wanted her. How much he craved her and how he'd missed her presence.

"Andrew," she whispered in the darkness. "Please."

He kissed her as he entered her tight heat.

Oh, God.

She moved with him and he knew that he was a lost man. Lana controlled his heart and mind—he needed her. He tried to formulate the words that he needed to say to her, the words that he wanted to say to her, but he couldn't say the words.

Instead he kissed her as their bodies joined together, moving together as one, and when she finally came around him, her fingers digging into his back, all he did was hold her closer to him as he came and kept the words to himself.

I love you.

CHAPTER FOURTEEN

WHEN LANA WOKE up it was because the sun was streaming hot on her face and the sheets were tangled around her legs. She rubbed her eyes as they adjusted to the sunlight and she reached out for Andrew, but his side of the bed was empty.

She sat up. “Andrew?”

There was no answer.

She got up and put on the nightgown that had been eventually discarded during their night of lovemaking. When she went out into the living room there was a note on the coffee table which was addressed to her.

Gone to the hospital. Making rounds. Didn’t want to wake you up.

Lana smiled as she folded the letter back up and got ready for the day. She had a shower and mulled over everything that had happened last night between them. When he’d first suggested they return to normal she'd agreed with him, though it stung.

Then she'd tossed and turned in her bed, missing his company.

She hated that she needed him to sleep. It was something she'd never needed before. She'd sworn when she moved out of her father's house and started to build a life for herself that she wouldn't rely on anyone else.

And then David had accused Andrew of using her, just like he'd used her.

As she was toweling herself off after her shower she could see perfect waves over the ocean. And as she stepped outside on the balcony the wind was blowing offshore and there were so many people out on boards, enjoying the pipelines.

Instead of putting on her clothes, she pulled on her board suit and braided her damp hair. She picked up her board and headed down to the beach. Her pulse was racing with anticipation. Lana rarely surfed, but when she did it always helped her see things clearly.

Her father hated that she loved it just as much as Jack did, but she did love it.

As she stood there Jack scrambled out of the

water, shaking his head from the surf. He saw her standing there and jogged over.

"How is it?" she asked.

"Choice," Jack said, panting.

"You ready for the championships in two weeks?"

He nodded. "Oh, yeah—you'll be there, right?"

"I'll be there."

"Good. I don't expect Dad will be there, huh?" Jack asked hopefully, but their dad never came to the surfing events, which were important to Jack.

"Doubtful."

"Have you talked to Sheila yet?"

"Who?" she asked, confused.

"Our mother." Jack's brow furrowed. "You should really talk to her."

Lana ignored him. She didn't want to discuss the person who'd abandoned them. "Are you too tired or are you going to come and surf with your sister for a bit?"

Jack rolled his eyes. "You're going surfing in your condition?"

"I'm not that far along. I'm fine. If I don't get it in now I won't be able to."

"Okay, you have a point. Yeah, let's go. I don't

want you to pearl yourself out there. Andrew would kick my butt if anything happened to you."

Lana snorted. "Yeah."

Jack stopped and smiled at her tenderly. "Yeah, he would, Lana. I don't know why you doubt yourself so much. You are worth it, but you don't see it and I don't get it."

Lana's heart swelled at her younger brother's tenderness and her emotions got the better of her. "Come on, before the wind changes direction and we lose the waves."

She waded out into the surf. The water was cold but it felt so good. She climbed onto her board and paddled out beside Jack. Her arms were noodling faster than they usually did, and the current was stronger than she was used to, but she swallowed her fear. She was going to conquer the pipeline today. Something she'd never been able to do.

As they continued to paddle she caught sight of the wave brewing. The wave that she'd tame today. She worked her arms hard and just as it began to crest she climbed on her board, catching the wave and popping up. She rode it, cycling herself in the pipeline, following the flow and motion of the water. She kept her balance and rode it, her soul screaming with joy, releasing every bit of tension and fear that she'd been carrying for so long. As she rode the pipeline, the turquoise water roaring in her ears and sparkling in the sunlight, she felt free for the first time in a long time.

As if nothing was going to stop her.

In that moment, while she conquered her fear of the big wave, she knew that she could conquer anything.

Even the thing she was scared of the most.

The pipeline shrank and she maneuvered her way out of it, crouching down and riding it until she was safe, out of harm's way. She dropped into the water, going under and breaking through the surface. A baptism of spirit and soul. Lana clung to her board and watched Jack riding another large pipeline. Only he didn't ride it so cautiously as she had done.

He was doing new school maneuvers that he would need to do in order to impress the judges at the International Surfing Championship in two weeks.

Jack was so free.

He didn't have any hang-ups and she envied

him that. She was envious of the life he led. He could go anywhere or do anything.

She had to stay here. Even more so now that she was expecting twins.

Here she had stability, a job and a home. She couldn't give that up to see the world. To practice medicine far away from Oahu.

With the twins, that dream had sailed.

Staying in Oahu was her only choice.

It's not. You're just afraid to try.

"What do you think, sis?" Jack asked, paddling up to her.

"It's great. You've got this, Jack."

Jack grinned proudly. "Do you want to catch another one?"

"No. I do have a job to do." She climbed on her board and paddled back to the shore. After climbing out of the buoyancy of the water, it felt as if she weighed a thousand pounds. Her body was completely exhausted.

She needed another shower before she headed to the hospital to make her rounds. When she tried to grab her board Jack took it from her.

"I got this, sis. You look tired. Go get ready for work. I'll take care of your board for you."

"Thank you, Keaka," she gently teased him.

He rolled his eyes but she kissed his cheek and headed back into the house, putting the ocean out of her mind.

Conquering that pipeline gave her a sense of accomplishment she hadn't felt in some time, but that would be something she would have to keep to herself.

Just a secret memory she could cling to when she needed to remind herself that she was doing the right thing, the safe thing, by staying in Oahu and eventually taking over her father's position.

She had more than herself to think of now.

"Dr. Tremblay speaking," Andrew said, answering the phone in his office.

No one spoke on the other end, but he could hear breathing and some background noise.

"Hello?" he asked, confused.

"Why did you call?"

The voice sent a shot of dread through him. He hadn't heard that voice in so long, except in his nightmares.

"Dad?" Andrew asked. "How did you get this number?"

"Why the hell did you call?" his father demanded once more; he was slurring.

Well, some things hadn't changed.

"I didn't call. You called me."

"Don't give me that crap. I know that you called her."

"Who?" Andrew asked with dread, hoping that his father wouldn't bring up his late sister. He didn't want to talk about Meghan, or the guilt he felt about that situation.

"Your mother. You called her. Why?"

"I never called Mom. Go drink another one." He slammed down the phone and it rang again. He ignored it, but it continued to ring over and over again.

"Hello," he said in a cautious tone, knowing full well who would be on the other end. His father began to cuss a blue streak at him.

"How dare you? Who do you think you are, hanging up on me? You killed your sister! How dare you call your mother?"

"I didn't call Mom." And then in the background he heard crying, his mother begging her husband to stop, and Andrew's heart broke. "Mom?"

"Don't you be talking to her!" his father screamed. "I saw you called from your fancy new home in Oahu. Told your mother you got married, eh, and that you're having a baby with your wife. I hope you don't ki—"

Andrew lost his cool. "Don't you even dare, old man. Don't you even dare imply that. I didn't kill Meghan. Our car hit a moose. She wasn't wearing a seat belt. It wasn't my fault. Being from the north, you, above all people, should know that! I couldn't save her. She was my sister, and it kills me to know that I couldn't help. That I had to leave her life in another surgeon's hands. Even if I could, by law, have operated on her she still would've died. I don't know why you care so much, though, when you were just as much of an asshole to her as you were to me. The only difference is she took it. She tried to keep the peace, to make you happy, to protect Mom, and you didn't care one bit because you were and are just a monster."

Andrew slammed down the phone again.

His hands were shaking—he was livid. He hadn't called his mother. She'd been weak and stuck by his father's side when he'd been disowned. She'd cut ties with him too, so why would he call her?

When they'd disowned him, he'd sworn that he would have nothing to do with them again.

So the question remained—who'd called them? Was it the senior Dr. Haole? Was it the hospital?

The hospital wouldn't tell your mother that you got married and were expecting twins.

"Hey," Lana said as she entered the office and shut the door. She stopped in her tracks when their eyes met. "Whoa, what happened?"

"Did you call my parents, by any chance?"

She bit her lip. "I know you told me not to, but you'd had surgery and…they had a right to know."

"God dammit, Iolana." He slammed his fist against the desk. "They had no right to know. They disowned me. I told you that. I didn't want them knowing anything about my life. They don't deserve to know."

"They're your parents," she snapped. "They should know."

"Oh? And have you told your mother what's happening? No, that's right, you dismissed her without hearing what she had to say."

Her eyes narrowed and her face was like thunder. "That's different."

"How?" Andrew demanded hotly. "How is it different?"

"My mother left when I was a child."

"And my parents left me when I was an adult. It's the same damn thing."

"Stop yelling at me. I was trying to help."

Andrew scrubbed a hand over his face. "Well, you screwed things up royally."

"And you're so perfect? So blameless?"

He leaned over the desk. "Are you insinuating that I'm at fault for my sister's death?"

"No, but you might as well be because of the way you carry it. You blame yourself. You believe them."

Andrew saw red, because she was right. She'd hit close to home.

Even though he wasn't responsible, he bore the burden. Every time he enjoyed an aspect of his life. Anytime he was close to being happy, he reminded himself of all that Meghan didn't ever get to experience. He'd been such a doofus most of his life and Meghan had always been so good. She didn't deserve to die.

He did. And he didn't deserve happiness.

"You need to leave, Lana," he said quietly. "You just have to go."

"I'm not going until we work this out."

"What is there to work out, Lana? This is a fake marriage. It'll be over in a year. I applied to a position in California before we were married and once my green card comes in I'm leaving Oahu. You'll never leave Oahu because who will take care of you then? Sorry I knocked you up, but you'll manage with your dad's help. If you can't take care of yourself, he can take care of you, which is what you let him do. You let him control you. You may strut around here like some kind of queen, but inside you're just a lost, lonely girl."

The slap stung his face.

And she didn't say another word to him. Just turned on her heel and walked out of his office. He held his hand up to where she'd struck him.

It burned. It hurt him right down to his core. The moment he'd said the words he regretted them, but it was for the best.

The words needed to be said.

There was no future for them because he didn't deserve one. At least his kids would be well taken care of.

They would be better off without him. He wasn't going to ruin Lana's life like he did Meghan's.

CHAPTER FIFTEEN

Two weeks later

LANA PICKED HER way through the crowd that had gathered in Waikiki for the International Surfing Championship. The wind was blowing offshore, which was making it perfect to catch waves. There were a lot of people from the International Surfing Commonwealth here. The ISC was where Andrew had applied to work. As soon as he got what he wanted, as soon as that green card came in, he was going to divorce her and head to California. She knew that.

But that's what you agreed to.

She couldn't think about Andrew. She hadn't seen him in two weeks and though she wanted to believe it didn't bother her, it did. There was a hole in her life. She was lonely, but he'd left her. So she was here for her brother, Jack. Not for Andrew, who had, as expected, crushed her heart so completely. She hated that she'd been right. That if she let herself fall in love with him he would break her heart.

And that was exactly what he'd done, but she supposed she'd had it coming to her.

She'd let her guard down and lost her heart. It was her fault. No one else was to blame but herself.

Now she had to make sure that her children were protected from Andrew, who apparently wanted nothing to do with them as he hadn't even shown up at the obstetrician appointment. That had hurt her.

What did you expect?

She had just been trying to help, to make the peace by stretching out an olive branch to Andrew's estranged parents.

Funny you can't extend the same olive branch to your own mother.

Lana found a shady spot, high in the stands, where she could see all of the action. She pulled out her binoculars and watched the competitors. On one of the boats that patrolled the water for injured surfers she caught sight of Andrew and her stomach clenched.

He was grinning and wearing an ISC red shirt. It suited him and he looked happy out there. And a bad niggling thought crept into her mind that he was probably happier without her.

Because when she'd got home that night two weeks ago, he'd already moved out.

"Next up is local surfer Keaka Jack Haole Jr., from the beautiful Waikiki. Give it up for ISC contender Keaka!" The announcement blasted over the crowd.

Lana cheered her brother, even though he wouldn't be able to hear her. She turned her binoculars over to the waves and caught sight of her brother and his bright neon-green surfboard. He caught a pipeline but wasn't in the hollow; he was riding it high as he did his tricks, much to the delight of the crowd.

He's going to win this.

And, just as he was about to perform a Shove-It, which was a tricky maneuver, his board flipped and he was tossed into the rocks.

Lana let out a cry and the boat with Andrew on board raced toward the rocks. She didn't waste time as she climbed down off the bleachers and started running for the beach.

Oh, God. Oh, God.

"I'm sorry, miss, you can't go past this point." A security guard barred her entrance to the beach.

"I'm a doctor and Keaka Haole is my brother."

The security guard let her past and she waited on the shore desperately.

It felt like an eternity that she waited.

She heard the distant sound of an ambulance making its way down the beach and then she saw the boat coming back from where Jack had been tossed. Lana waded out in the water after the boat stopped in the shallows. She could see Andrew had Jack strapped to a back board. There was blood everywhere and, just from a quick assessment, her brother was pretty mangled.

"Oh, God," she whispered as she ran forward.

"Lana, you need to step back," Andrew said gently. "It's bad."

Lana ignored him and helped carry the back board through the water. This was her brother, who she'd raised. He was all she had, the only man who had ever really seen her. She couldn't lose her only ally in this world.

"Lana, I got this," Andrew snapped.

"He's my brother. I don't care how bad it is. I'm not leaving his side," she snapped back. "I'm here, Jack. I'm here."

The paramedics took over and Andrew began to bark orders as they did the ABCs on Jack and started a central line. Jack was unconscious but breathing, but his trachea had been damaged, so they were inserting a tube.

Lana felt powerless as she knelt next to her brother in the sand, her hands covered in his blood.

The only man who really understood her. Who loved her. She couldn't lose him. She would be lost without her brother.

"It's okay, Jack. I'm here. I'm here."

The paramedics got him stabilized and strapped down onto a gurney to take him to the hospital. They loaded him into the back and Andrew followed, but when Lana tried to climb in the paramedic stopped her.

"Sorry, miss. Only family."

"It's okay, she's his sister and she's a surgeon," Andrew said.

The paramedic nodded and helped Lana up, shutting the door and then climbing into the front, while another paramedic in the back continued to monitor Jack.

"Thank you," Lana said quickly, not looking at Andrew, because she couldn't look at the man who'd broken her heart.

"You're welcome." Then he raked a hand through his hair. "Lana, there's… Look, I…"

"No, I don't want to talk about it, Andrew." She shook her head. "Not now. My brother is clinging to life and that's all that matters."

Andrew nodded.

She kept her focus on Jack during the ride to the hospital. Which felt like an eternity.

Once the ambulance door opened she jumped out and ran into the trauma department.

"Someone page my father to Trauma, stat!" she shouted.

Dr. Page, one of the residents, ran off to a phone and Lana turned back to the paramedics wheeling Jack in. Andrew was helping them.

"Page a trauma surgeon," Andrew shouted. He was barking orders as they wheeled Jack into a trauma pod. A crash cart was pushed into the room and Andrew was putting on a gown. All Lana could do was stand back and watch in horror as the paramedics handed Jack over to Andrew and the trauma surgeon, Dr. Rodman, who had come rushing into the pod.

"Iolana, what's going on?" her father said as he came rushing toward the pod. Then his eyes widened in shock. "You're covered in blood!"

"It's not me," Lana said and she held her father back. "It's Jack. A wave tossed him and it's bad, Dad. It's really bad."

Her father raked a hand through his hair. "I told him not do it. I told him it was dangerous."

"Yeah, but he loves it, Dad! He did something he's passionate about, just like you. You two are so alike."

Her father snorted. "We are not alike, Lana."

"You are both exactly alike. You're stubborn, unbending and you both nag me until you get what you want!"

Her father's eyes widened as the words came out of her mouth.

"I raised Jack so I know that he's like you. He just did what he felt passionately about. Just because he didn't follow your path doesn't mean that his path wasn't right."

"His path led him to this, Iolana. He might die!" her father shouted.

"And he dies loving what he was doing. I was too busy trying to keep the peace between you two, to take care of Jack when you were working doing what you loved, I sacrificed most of my life to give you both what you wanted."

"You love surgery…"

"I do, but I wanted to leave Oahu. Dad, you left us." She was tired of holding it all in. Tired of pretending. She wasn't just angry at her mother; she was angry at him too for controlling her life.

"I didn't leave you," her father said darkly. "Your mother left."

"She left physically, but you weren't there either, Dad. I raised Jack. I didn't have a childhood."

Her father's head hung. "I couldn't be home."

"Why? We needed you and you weren't there," she said.

"It was too hard. I loved your mother and she left us. Home was a reminder of my broken heart."

Tears welled in her eyes. "I loved her too, but we needed you, Dad. And I'm sorry we're such a disappointment to you. Such a burden"

"You're not. You weren't. I'm sorry."

She nodded and then swallowed her fear to tell him more. She was tired of lying. "Jack had me marry Andrew for a green card."

"What?" her father demanded. "Iolana..."

She held up her hand. "At first, but I fell in love with Andrew. I want these babies. Don't be mad at Andrew or Jack. It was my decision, it was my mistake and I'm owning it, but I have to take charge of my own life, Dad, and you need to be more supportive of Jack. I can't be the peace-keeper between the two of you anymore. I'm done. It's time I get to live my own life. I can't follow in your shadow any longer."

Her father was taken aback by her outburst and so was she, to be honest. "Iolana?"

Then she broke down in tears and her father pulled her close, holding her and comforting her the way he had never done. The last time she'd embraced her father it was when he'd been crying because her mother had left and she had held him while he cried. Now he was holding her, because she was terrified.

A code blue was called and she could hear Andrew shouting over the fray as Dr. Rodman shocked her brother as he coded.

"Oh, God, I can't lose my son! I can't." Her father broke down. "Please, God, no."

Lana held onto her father tighter and then, as Jack's heart stabilized, she knew exactly who she had to call, but she was afraid to do it.

Andrew came out of the trauma pod. His face was grim.

"What's going on?" her father demanded.

"He's stabilized, but it's not good. They're taking him down to do a CT scan right now. Dr. Rodman is an excellent trauma surgeon and he'll be able to tell us the extent of the damage."

Her father nodded. "I'm going to go down with him."

"Okay, but Dr. Haole, remember that Dr. Rodman is the surgeon. Not you. You can't interfere."

"I know," her father said quietly and he left Lana and Andrew standing in the hall as he followed Jack's gurney down for an emergency CT scan.

She turned to leave, but Andrew grabbed her arm and dragged her into a private room. He discarded the trauma gown and washed his hands.

"Why did you bring me in here?" she demanded. "I should be with Jack and my father."

"They're fine. It's you I'm worried about. You and the babies."

"Could've fooled me," she snapped.

"I know I didn't go to that obstetrician appointment. I'm sorry. I was angry and scared."

"And now?" she asked, crossing her arms.

"I don't know. Worried. I'm worried about my friend."

"Yes, Jack has been a good friend to you. Got

you hooked up with his sister so you could land your cushy job with the ISC."

"Lana, you know that's always been my dream."

"So you were offered a job?" she asked.

"No, not yet, but if I am I'm going to take it and if you weren't so scared you could come with me."

"Why would I go with you?"

"You wouldn't. I know you wouldn't."

Before she could answer, Dr. Page, the orthopedic resident, stuck his head in the room. "Sorry to interrupt, Dr. Tremblay, but Dr. Haole is requesting you come down to the CT scan. They have results and they need you down there, stat."

Andrew nodded. "I'll be right there. Thank you, Dr. Page."

Dr. Page left and Andrew turned back to her. "This isn't over. We need to talk."

Lana didn't say anything else. Andrew left the room and the room began to spin as the adrenaline of what'd happened began to wear off.

There was a phone on the wall and she knew what she had to do. She left the trauma department and made her way up to her office. It was a Saturday so her assistant Kelley wasn't there.

Which was good. She had to pull herself together to tackle what she was going to do. There was a card on her desk. One that had been left when her mother had come to see her a month ago.

With trembling hands she picked up the phone and dialed the number.

"Hello?" It was the voice she recalled from when she was a girl. Before her mother left, the gentle voice that had sung her Hawaiian lullabies to calm the night terrors. The voice that had haunted her for years, until it faded into the recesses of her memory after she'd left. Now it was all rushing back and she had to keep her voice calm.

"It's Iolana," she managed to say.

"Iolana, I'm so glad you called me!" Her voice was genuine. She was happy and now Iolana had to break the news to her.

"I have bad news," she choked back.

"What is it?"

"It's Keaka… I mean it's Jack. He's been in an accident. It's not looking good. You should prepare yourself."

There was a strangled cry on the other end. "Oh, my God. I'm coming. Hold on. I'll be there soon."

"I'll meet you at the ER doors." Lana disconnected the call. Her hand still shaking, she buried her face in her hands and wept.

Things were going to change.

Life was too short.

"His pelvis and his hip are fractured. His femur is also broken, all on the left side. It's like his body was crushed on one side only. There is a fracture of some of the right ribs, but those aren't as serious as the pelvis, hip and femur," Andrew said, pointing to the images that were on the computer. "The pelvis is crushed on this side and he has extensive internal bleeding."

Dr. Rodman nodded. "I need to get him into the OR and control the bleeding."

"Agreed, and once the bleeding is stabilized his bones need to be repaired. As long as he can tolerate it. We'll see how he does after you stop the bleeding."

Dr. Rodman left the CT room and went to speak to Dr. Haole. Jack needed to go straight into surgery.

Andrew just stared up at the screen and had the other two orthopedic surgeons paged. One was in the OR doing a hip replacement and the other was away at a conference.

Dr. Haole couldn't perform the surgery because he was Jack's father and Lana couldn't perform this surgery either.

He broke out in a cold sweat.

"It's bad?" Lana asked as she came into the CT room.

Andrew nodded. "I'm sorry. You can see the extent of his injuries. When he hit the rocks, it crushed the left side of his body."

Lana nodded, but kept her calm. "He'll need extensive work."

"Right, and one surgeon is in the operating room and the other is at a conference, which just leaves..."

"You," she said as a matter of fact. "You've been cleared for surgery. You're one of the best orthopedic surgeons, Andrew. Dad can't do it. I can't. There's only you. My other two orthopedic surgeons are fine, they're good, but I want the best working on my brother. It has to be you."

"I can't, Lana..." Which was pathetic. He had to, but he was terrified in that moment. It had been four years since he'd picked up a scalpel and operated on a patient. His first patient couldn't be his friend, the brother of the woman he loved.

"You have to," she snapped. "I want the best for my brother. Save his life."

"What if I can't? It's been four years, Lana. And if he dies… I know I've screwed up, but if he dies I can't lose you."

Lana didn't say anything for a moment. Then she grabbed him by his shoulders. "You've got this. I'm not your parents. You won't lose me, unless you walk away from this."

Andrew pulled her into his arms and kissed her. Terrified about what he was about to do, not fully believing that his hand wouldn't shake, that Lana wouldn't walk away if Jack didn't survive. But she was right—if he walked away Jack would die and he would lose her.

He couldn't lose her.

And their two weeks apart, when he'd left, had been brutal. He'd missed her and he realized how lonely his life had become. He wanted Lana, but he was worried that he'd blown it. Now he had a way to make it all right.

And he would make sure that after all was said and done he'd win her over.

And he would never leave again.

CHAPTER SIXTEEN

LANA WAITED FOR her mother, her insides turning as she paced. Jack was in the operating room with the trauma surgeon and Andrew was in the skills lab with his resident, Dr. Page, trying to come up with a game plan on how to save her brother.

Jack.

He was still alive, she could feel it, but if she lost her brother she didn't know what she'd do. And then she had an inkling of what Andrew must've felt when his sister died in the accident. Jack had always been someone she could rely on when they were growing up.

He butted heads with her father constantly, but Jack was always there for her. He gave her the hugs she'd craved from her parents, the unquestioning love, and, though he drove her nuts, she couldn't imagine her life without him.

Just like she couldn't imagine her life without Andrew.

Love had crept up on her so fast and stealthily. It was something she wasn't expecting, but it was there nonetheless and Jack's accident made her realize that she couldn't be the moderator in her family's life any longer.

There would be hurt, pain, but also happiness. She couldn't live her life anymore to keep the peace. She had to live her life for herself.

She had to do what made her happy. She had to not act like a strong woman, but be one. Be the one she knew was in there. So when Andrew left for California, if he wanted her to, she would go with him and their kids.

Lana was tired of living the life her father deemed appropriate. It was now time to live the life she wanted and take it.

The doors to the emergency room slid open and her mother came in, this time not in a business suit but yoga pants, running shoes and a hoodie. Her silver hair brushed back and those blue eyes filled with pain and worry.

"Iolana," her mother whispered as she came forward, as if to hug her, but then thought better of it and stood back.

"Mom," Lana said and then pulled the woman she'd been mourning since she was ten and held tight to her. Like she should've done when she'd come in that first time a month ago. Her mother broke down in sobs as she clutched her tight. As if she didn't want to let her go.

"Iolana… Oh, God."

"It's okay, Mom. It's okay." They broke apart and Lana took her mother's hand and led her to her father's office, where he was waiting.

As soon as she opened the door, her father spun around and saw the tears. "Not Jack. No."

"No, Dad. It's not Jack. Not directly." Lana turned to her mother and pushed her into the room.

Her father's expression softened and then hardened. "Sheila."

"Keaka," her mother said in the same tone. There was no love lost there.

"What're you doing here?" her father demanded.

"Iolana called me. I'm here because our son is in the operating room."

Her dad shot Lana a look, which would usually have her contrite, but instead she crossed her arms and stared him down.

"She did, did she? I don't know why you bothered to come here now, after all these years. Your son won't care that you're here."

"Yes, Dad, he will," Lana snapped. "Jack has been talking to Mom for over a month. He's made amends."

"You knew about this?" Her dad bellowed.

"Don't bully her," her mother said, stepping between them. "You were always a blow hard."

"You left. You gave up your rights to these kids."

"I left because we didn't love each other. I left because I was suffering from severe postpartum depression. It took me many years to heal myself and, if you recall, I've tried to come back but you've turned me away."

Now her dad looked contrite.

"Jack wants her here, Dad. So do I." Lana turned to her mother. "I want to make amends too."

Her mother smiled and took her hand. "I want that too, Iolana. More than anything."

Lana nodded and turned to her father. "I love you, Dad, but as I said I'm tired of being the peacekeeper between you and Jack. I'm tired of having my life dictated to me."

"I only did those things because it would be better for you," her father said. "You had a talent for surgery. You needed to be here so I could pass on my gift."

She took her father's hand. "And I thank you for that gift, Dad, but it's time to let me go. It's time to let me live my life. Even if it means that I don't make the choices you would want. I'm not going to be a stay-at-home mother. I'm going to continue performing surgery. I want my kids to see a strong woman and I love surgery, but I don't want to be Chief of Surgery when you retire. I want to work for the International Surfing Commonwealth. I want to do research, maybe even teach medicine. The options are endless, but I have to leave Hawaii to do that."

"What are you saying?" he asked suspiciously.

"Andrew has applied for a job in California and if he gets it I'm going to go with him."

"Do you know if that's what he wants?" her father asked. "You may love him but, as you said, you married him to get him a green card. He may not want you to come."

She sighed. "That's a risk I'll have to take, but I know that I can't live under your wings. I have to step out of your shadow. You have to let me go. And you have to stop fighting with Jack because he decided to live the life he wants and not the life you designed for him. And you have to bury the hatchet with Mom. I want both of you in my children's lives and I know Jack wants you both in his life. He will have a tough road to hoe. Lots of physical therapy after his surgery. He's doesn't need your condemnation for his life-style choices. He needs your support. He'll need it from you both!"

Her father didn't say anything.

"Now, I'm going to check on Jack and leave you two to talk it through. You need to put your past hurts aside and move on. For Jack. For me."

"Very well, Iolana." Her father kissed her on the top of the head and her mother nodded, but eyed her father warily.

Lana left her father's office, shutting the door and telling his administrative assistant not to let anyone disturb him.

Sophie came running up then, out of breath. "Lana, I just heard about Jack. How is Keaka handling it?"

"Well, I think." Lana took her stepmother aside. "Sophie, I want you to know I love you. I've always thought of you as a mother."

Sophie gasped. "Oh, no. What's happening?"

“My mother is in there and is making peace with Dad. For Jack’s sake.”

Sophie sighed in relief. “I’m so glad.”

“You don’t seem surprised.”

“I’m not. I’ve known Sheila for three years. She works on the Waikiki arts council and I worked with her for a fund-raiser. How do you think she got the information about you and Jack?”

Lana chuckled. “So you knew?”

“Of course. This has been a long time coming and I’m glad.” Then she pushed an errant strand of hair off Lana’s face. “I love you too. I never had kids of my own, but I think of you and Jack like mine.”

They hugged and Lana held her tight, because even though Sophie had been a wonderful maternal figure through her later teen years, Lana had never embraced her before and it was highly overdue. Especially since Sophie had been instrumental in bringing her and her mother back together. For healing the pain that Lana had been feeling since her mother had walked away. If she hadn’t been so blind to it in the first place, it might’ve saved some pain in the past.

“I’ll leave them to work it out and head to the cafeteria for some coffee after I leave a message for your father. Where are you off to?" Sophie asked.

"The gallery. I'm going to watch Jack's surgery."

"Is that wise?" Sophie asked.

"Yeah, Jack needs to know I'm there. And so does Andrew."

Sophie nodded. "Text me if there are any changes."

"I will." She kissed Sophie's cheek and then left.

She needed to be in that gallery. She needed to be there if something happened to Jack. Not that her presence would help, but she wanted to be there nonetheless.

She wanted him to know that she was there for him. And she wanted Andrew to know that she supported him, whatever happened in that OR. She wanted Andrew to know that she was there for him and she always would be.

There would be no more running away. She was in this for the long haul.

"You could've saved her! You killed her!"

Andrew rolled his shoulders out of habit from years of pain, now it was to loosen them up. He wasn't quite a month post-op from his surgery, but his hand had stayed stable in the skills lab until Dr. Rodman paged him. There was still work to be done, but they would work together. Dr. Rodman would address the injuries to the organs in the abdomen and thoracic area and Andrew would work on the pelvis, hip and femur.

Jack's left arm had been severely fractured too, but that could wait.

There would be several surgeries over the next little while.

It would be a long road to hoe, but what was most devastating was that Jack probably would never surf again. Maybe now Jack would get his head out of his butt and go to school to become a kinesiologist, like he said he wanted to do after he retired from surfing.

And Andrew was going to support his friend, who was now his family. As long as he didn't screw up this surgery. As long as Jack survived, because he just couldn't believe that Lana would ever be able to look at him again without thinking that he couldn't save her little brother.

And it made him think about his children that Lana was carrying, his twin babies.

There was no other option. He would succeed.

Please let him live.

Andrew took a deep breath and headed into the OR. No words were needed; he knew what had to happen. He knew where he was going to start first. He was going to repair the pelvis, where most of the internal bleeding had been coming from. Once the pelvis was stable, then he would move onto the hip and femur, as long as Jack was able to stand it.

The arm could be fixed later if needed. And the ribs would knit themselves back together. A nurse held out a surgical gown, which Andrew slipped into. And then into the gloves. His pulse began to race and he rolled his shoulder again.

He glanced up into the gallery. Lana was there, watching, and this time, instead of him giving her a nod of encouragement, she did.

Andrew took his spot and took a calming breath. "Hold that retractor tight, I will need a lot of room to maneuver the pelvis. Is the hardware ready?"

"Yes, Dr. Tremblay," Dr. Page said. "I brought an assortment for all the fractures. I also have an external fixture ready."

"Good man." Andrew picked up a surgical

drill. "Let's go. We have to get Jack back up on his feet."

And as he went to work he felt as if his sister was right there. One of the injuries she'd sustained was a pelvic fracture when the moose crashed through the windshield and landed on her. Her pelvis had been shattered and she'd lost a lot of blood, but ultimately it was the head injury that did her in.

Jack's head hadn't sustained an injury. There were no bleeds in his brain.

Which was a miracle, but blood loss, a clot or being under too long could be detrimental to him.

I got this, Jack. You're not going anywhere.

He tuned the world out and instead he heard his sister whispering that he was going to succeed, that she loved him and that he was a good surgeon.

It wasn't Andrew's fault that she'd died. Just like it wasn't Lana's fault that Jack was injured. Meghan had been an adult and had chosen not to buckle up that night. No one was at fault and Andrew deserved to have happiness.

He deserved to have Lana.

"You do," Meghan's voice said in his head.

Like a blessing from beyond. His own guardian angel watching out for him. It calmed him.

Even if he'd messed it up royally, he was going to earn Lana's love back. He couldn't lose her. He needed her. He needed their kids. And he would do anything to be with her, even if it meant giving up the job with the International Surfing Commonwealth in San Diego because Lana wanted to stay in Hawaii with her family.

He didn't care. He just wanted to be with her. Whatever it took.

He was tired of living alone. Tired of thinking that he didn't deserve happiness.

He wanted a family.

He wanted Lana.

Lana went to check on her brother. He was still in a medicated coma, but he'd survived and the bleeding had stopped. Tomorrow Andrew was going to go in and fix the fractures in Jack's left arm and shoulder, which had dislocated.

The pelvis and hip had been repaired and was being held together with an external fixator. The femur had been repaired with some heavy-duty hardware.

But the point was, he was going to live.

Jack was very lucky to be alive.

Andrew was standing at the foot of the bed, filling out Jack's chart while Dr. Page waited diligently for instructions. Dr. Page was the resident on call for Jack tonight and she couldn't have picked a better resident herself.

Andrew handed over the chart and then left the room. His eyes widened in surprise when he saw her.

"Lana, I thought you went home! It's the middle of the night."

"I had a nap in my office and some food. Don't worry. I'm taking care of myself."

Andrew nodded. He was going to say something, but then her parents came down the hall. Her father didn't say anything; he just patted Andrew on the back and nodded. Her father, Sophie and Lana's mother all filtered into the room.

Lana stood at the doorway, watching, as her father broke down in tears and took Jack's hand. Sophie and Lana's mother held hands and Lana sighed happily. Then she turned to Andrew.

"Thank you," she said.

"For what?" he asked.

"For saving Jack's life. I know that was hard for you."

"It was, I won't lie, but… I couldn't let him die."

"You didn't let your sister die, Andrew."

He took her hand then and pulled her into an empty on call room and locked the door. He crossed his arms and she could tell he was struggling.

"I couldn't let him die, because I didn't want to lose you." He stared at her intently. "I couldn't lose you. I know I screwed up when I walked out…"

She cupped his face. "You wouldn't have lost me. I know it was out of your hands. You weren't at fault for your sister's death and I wouldn't have blamed you if Jack had died."

"I love you, Iolana," he said quickly. "It's been hard for me to say, but I love you more than anything and the thought of losing you forever, the thought of you walking away from me like my parents did, of not seeing your face every day—it was more than I could bear."

Tears streamed down her face. "I love you too, Andrew. I'm sorry for calling your mother. I just wanted to make amends. I thought if you could make peace with your estranged family then you could move forward."

Andrew took her in his arms and kissed her,

making her weak in the knees. "Lana, they may not want me, but it doesn't matter. All I want is you. You showed me what I was missing, what I didn't think that I deserved. I'm a better man because of you and I won't lose you again."

"I love you, Andrew. I never believed in love. I didn't think I wanted this, but I do and when you're offered a job with the ISC I'll go to San Diego with you." She chuckled softly. "I mean *we'll* come with you."

"No, I was going to turn down the ISC job. You belong here in Hawaii."

"No, I don't. I was afraid to leave because I was afraid to step out of my father's shadow. There's so much beyond Hawaii. There's so much more life to live and if I can be with you I would follow you to the ends of the earth."

"Ditto," he teased and then kissed her again. "So you want to move to California after my green card gets in and I can move legally?"

She nodded. "Let's go. Let's live our life. One that we decide."

He grinned. "It's a deal. What does your father think?"

"It doesn't matter what he thinks. All that matters is that we're together. The four of us."

"You're right. That's all that matters. I love you, Iolana." And then he reached down and touched her stomach. "I love all three of you. And I will make it up to you."

"Make up what to me?" she questioned.

"As soon as possible we're going to renew our wedding vows, because this time I really mean it. The last time we got married, we did it to keep me in the country, but this time I want it to mean something. When I marry you again, it'll be because I can't imagine my life without you."

"Andrew, we don't need to get married again. Once was enough, but just knowing how you feel now is enough for me. There's no way I'm stuffing myself back into that dress."

A smile crept across his face. "Okay, no wedding renewal, but how about a repeat of the wedding night?"

She laughed and wrapped her arms around his neck. "Now that I can handle, Dr. Tremblay. Gladly."

After he kissed her again to give her a preview of what she could expect, they went hand in hand to visit Jack and be with their family.

And to break the news that they would be leaving after the babies were born, so they could start their life together.

For real this time.

EPILOGUE

One year later, San Diego

ANDREW RAN ACROSS the road, under the bridge. The palm trees were swaying and he hoped that the wind whipping down from the mountains wouldn't delay the flight that was coming in.

Lana was on her cell phone and waiting outside.

Even though it was windy, it was a nice day and in the double stroller were two babies who were almost six months old and just starting to be aware of their surroundings. Two little girls who were almost identical except Meghan had brown eyes and Jackie had blue. Right now they were staring up at the sky, at the palm fronds and the roar of the planes as they came in for landing over the city.

Lana ended the call. "Did you get the car parked okay?"

"Yeah. Why did we have to come so early again?"

"To get a good spot," she said.

"But I can just drive in the loop and do a pick-up."

Lana narrowed her eyes. "I am not greeting your mother by myself, so since you can't park in the loop you can get a good parking spot out there."

Andrew knelt down to his smiling happy babies. "Your mother is crazy!"

"Ha-ha," she said.

"Who was on the phone?" he asked as he took the helm of the large double stroller.

"Jack."

"Oh? And did he get into the school of his choice?"

"He did, so there's some good news and bad news."

Andrew's stomach clenched. "What?"

"He got into his first choice of school to become a kinesiologist."

"Right?" Andrew asked cautiously.

"It's here in San Diego and he's going to move in with us."

Andrew started laughing. "Are you serious?

Where are we going to put him at the beach house?"

"There's the little bunkie out back by the hot tub and the pool. It has a bathroom. He can live there."

"He just wants to use our hot tub again. Just like he did when we lived in Waikiki. I say we move back now that he's coming here."

Lana laughed. "Dad would love that, but where would we work? Dad retired and is travelling the world with Sophie. Mom is busy with the art council and Dr. Rodman is Chief."

"Dr. Rodman would hire us both back in a minute."

She rolled her eyes but laughed. "You just got promoted at the ISC and I just started teaching medical students at the University of California. We're happy here—do you really want to move back to Hawaii?"

He grinned and then kissed her on the lips. "Sometimes, because I think of those few nights we spent on the Big Island for our second honeymoon."

Lana wrapped her arms around his waist and pulled him closer. "You know, maybe it's time for the girls to have a brother?"

"I'm willing to try for that, but I think we have more than we can handle with these two. But I'm really game for trying."

And he forgot that he was at the airport as he pressed Lana up against the wall, trapping her there as he thought about their second honeymoon and their private hideaway. A howl from one of the girls brought him back to reality.

"The flight's probably landed. Let's go," he said reluctantly. He pushed the stroller into the arrivals lounge at San Diego Airport and waited near the luggage carousel, his eyes trained on the escalator for the arriving passengers to make their way down.

He was nervous and as if she sensed that Lana took his hand and gave it a squeeze.

"You got this."

"I know, it took a lot of guts for her to come here." Then he glanced at the board and saw that the flight from Toronto had landed. "I still can't believe that she left him. I can't believe that she called me."

"She was powerless, you know that, and she wants to bridge the gap. She's obviously realized that by staying with your father she lost out on so much."

Andrew nodded, but he was nervous all the same.

When his mother had called it had shocked him. She had left his father soon after his father had called him and ranted at him. She'd gone to a women's shelter to try and piece back together her life. Three months ago his father had been killed in an accident; it had been his fault and thankfully no one else had been hurt.

Andrew had hated leaving Lana to go to Canada, but he'd needed to go and bury his father, to bury his past. His green card had come in and he was able to go back to Canada.

That was where he and his mother had reconnected, but there was still a lot of healing to do. Finally, his mother was able to come to San Diego for a long visit and to see her grandchildren, which was why she'd left his father.

She wanted to be a grandmother more than anything. She was tired of living in the past—one full of bitterness, abuse and sorrow.

Andrew's mother wanted her family back.

And he wanted his mother back.

A bunch of people started to come down the

escalators and he let go of Lana's hand to take a step forward, scanning the crowd.

Maybe she didn't come.

And then he saw her. Saw the long silver hair, the weary face, but she smiled and waved when she spotted him and his heart soared.

She got off the escalator, pulling a carry-on behind her.

"Mom, I'm glad you made it."

His mother reached up and pulled him into a hug. When he'd been up for his father's funeral, his mother had been stand-offish and in shock. He understood that. She'd never been an affectionate woman so he was taken aback by the hug now, but he loved it all the same.

"Andrew, I've missed you," she whispered.

"I'm so glad you've come, Mom. I've missed you too." He broke off the embrace and looked down at his mother. The blue eyes—the same that his late sister had, that he had and his daughter Jackie had. He turned. "This is Lana, my wife."

His mother didn't say much but embraced Lana, kissing her, and then knelt down, crying, as she looked at the babies.

"They're so beautiful," she whispered as she

took a chubby fist into her hand. "Just as I imagined them. Which one is which?"

"The best way to tell them apart is Meghan has brown eyes," Lana said. "And Jackie has blue."

"So they do. Oh, now I see the difference in them." She stood. "Thank you for having me come here. I've… I've wanted to come for some time, but it's been hard."

"I know, Mom, and we're glad to have you here too. Do you have any more luggage?"

"No, just a carry-on. I wasn't left with much in the way of personal belongings." She blushed, embarrassed.

"That doesn't matter, Mom. You're welcome to stay as long as you want."

"Well, Customs in Canada said to buy a return ticket home, an open-ended one, as long as I return in six months."

"We would love to have you for as long as you want to stay, Annie," Lana said.

"Thank you, dear. Six months is a start. I don't fancy getting a green card the way you did, Andrew," she teased. "I'm glad you did it that way, though. You have a beautiful family."

Lana smiled up at Andrew and he put his arms around his mother and his wife, as he looked down at his girls. One who was cooing and one who was drifting off to sleep in the stroller. The hole that had been aching in his heart for years, another pain that he'd gotten used to over time, was finally healed.

Now his heart was bursting with joy.

"I do have a beautiful family. I have all I ever wanted."

And he walked out of that airport complete.

* * * * *